Lives of the English Poets: Prior, Congreve, Blackmore, Pope

Samuel Johnson

Contents

LIVES OF THE ENGLISH POETS: PRIOR, CONGREVE, BLACKMORE,

POPE

BY

Samuel Johnson

INTRODUCTION

When, at the age of sixty-eight, Johnson was writing these "Lives of the English Poets," he had caused omissions to be made from the poems of Rochester, and was asked whether he would allow the printers to give all the verse of Prior. Boswell quoted a censure by Lord Hailes of "those impure tales which will be the eternal opprobrium of their ingenious author." Johnson replied, "Sir, Lord Hailes has forgot. There is nothing in Prior that will excite to lewdness;" and when Boswell further urged, he put his questionings aside, and added, "No, sir, Prior is a lady's book. No lady is ashamed to have it standing in her library." Johnson distinguished strongly, as every wise man does, between offence against convention, and offence against morality.

In Congreve's plays he recognised the wit but condemned the morals, and in the case of Blackmore the regard for the religious purpose of Blackmore's poem on "The Creation" gave to Johnson, as to Addison, an undue sense of its literary value.

With his "Life of Pope," which occupies more than two-thirds of this volume, Johnson took especial pains. "He wrote it," says Boswell, "'con amore,' both from the early possession which that writer had taken of his mind, and from the pleasure which he must have felt in for ever silencing all attempts to lessen his poetical fame. . . . I remember once to have heard Johnson say, 'Sir, a thousand years may elapse before there shall appear another man with a power of versification equal to that of Pope.'"

Pope's laurel, since Johnson's days, has flourished, without showing a dead bough, for all the frosts of hostile criticism.

H. M.

PRIOR

Matthew Prior is one of those that have burst out from an obscure original to great eminence. He was born July 21, 1664, according to some, at Wimborne, in Dorsetshire, of I know not what parents; others say that he was the son of a joiner of London: he was perhaps willing enough to leave his birth unsettled, in hope, like Don Quixote, that the historian of his actions might find him some illustrious alliance. He is supposed to have fallen, by his father's death, into the hands of his uncle, a vintner near Charing Cross, who sent him for some time to Dr. Busby, at Westminster; but, not intending to give him any education beyond that of the school, took him, when he was well advanced in literature, to his own house, where the Earl of Dorset, celebrated for patronage of genius, found him by chance, as Burnet relates, reading Horace, and was so well pleased with his proficiency, that he undertook the care and cost of his academical education. He entered his name in St. John's College, at Cambridge, in 1682, in his eighteenth year; and it may be reasonably supposed that he was distinguished among his contemporaries. He became a Bachelor, as is usual, in four years, and two years afterwards wrote the poem on the Deity, which stands first in his volume.

It is the established practice of that College to send every year to the Earl of Exeter some poems upon sacred subjects, in acknowledgment of a benefaction enjoyed by them from the bounty of his ancestor. On this occasion were those verses written, which, though nothing is said of their success, seem to have recommended him to some notice; for his praise of the countess's music, and his lines on the famous picture of Seneca, afford reason for imagining that he was more or less conversant with that family.

The same year he published "The City Mouse and Country Mouse," to ridicule

Dryden's "Hind and Panther," in conjunction with Mr. Montague. There is a story of great pain suffered, and of tears shed, on this occasion by Dryden, who thought it hard that "an old man should be so treated by those to whom he had always been civil." By tales like these is the envy raised by superior abilities every day gratified. When they are attacked every one hopes to see them humbled; what is hoped is readily believed, and what is believed is confidently told. Dryden had been more accustomed to hostilities than that such enemies should break his quiet; and, if we can suppose him vexed, it would be hard to deny him sense enough to conceal his uneasiness.

"The City Mouse and Country Mouse" procured its authors more solid advantages than the pleasure of fretting Dryden, for they were both speedily preferred. Montague, indeed, obtained the first notice with some degree of discontent, as it seems, in Prior, who probably knew that his own part of the performance was the best. He had not, however, much reason to complain, for he came to London and obtained such notice that (in 1691) he was sent to the Congress at the Hague as secretary to the embassy. In this assembly of princes and nobles, to which Europe has perhaps scarcely seen anything equal, was formed the grand alliance against Louis, which at last did not produce effects proportionate so the magnificence of the transaction.

The conduct of Prior, in this splendid initiation into public business, was so pleasing to King William, that he made him one of the gentlemen of his bedchamber; and he is supposed to have passed some of the next years in the quiet cultivation of literature and poetry.

The death of Queen Mary (in 1695) produced a subject for all the writers--perhaps no funeral was ever so poetically attended. Dryden, indeed, as a man discountenanced and deprived, was silent; but scarcely any other maker of verses omitted to bring his tribute of tuneful sorrow. An emulation of elegy was universal. Mary's praise was not confined to the English language, but fills a great part of the Musae Anglicanae.

Prior, who was both a poet and a courtier, was too diligent to miss this opportunity of respect. He wrote a long ode, which was presented to the king, by whom it was not likely to be ever read. In two years he was secretary to another embassy at the Treaty of Ryswick (in 1697), and next year had the same office at the court of France, where he is said to have been considered with great distinction. As he was one day surveying the apartments at Versailles, being shown the "Victories of Louis," painted by Le Brun, and asked whether the King of England's palace had any such decorations: "The monuments of my master's actions," said he, "are to be seen everywhere but in his own house."

The pictures of Le Brun are not only in themselves sufficiently ostentatious, but were explained by inscriptions so arrogant, that Boileau and Racine thought it necessary to make them more simple. He was in the following year at Leo with the king, from whom, after a long audience, he carried orders to England, and upon his arrival became Under Secretary of State in the Earl of Jersey's office, a post which he did not retain long, because Jersey was removed, but he was soon made Commissioner of Trade.

This year (1700) produced one of his longest and most splendid compositions, the "Carmen Seculare," in which he exhausts all his powers of celebration. I mean not to accuse him of flattery; he probably thought all that he writ, and retained as much veracity as can be properly exacted from a poet professedly encomiastic. King William supplied copious materials for either verse or prose. His whole life had been action, and none ever denied him the resplendent qualities of steady resolution and personal courage. He was really in Prior's mind what he represents him in his verses; he considered him as a hero, and was accustomed to say that he praised others in compliance with the fashion, but that in celebrating King William he followed his inclination. To Prior, gratitude would dictate praise, which reason would not refuse.

Among the advantages to arise from the future years of William's reign, he mentions a Society for Useful Arts, and among them:-

"Some that with care true eloquence shall teach, And to just idioms fix our doubtful speech; That from our writers distant realms may know   The thanks we to our monarchs owe, And schools profess our tongue through every land That has invoked his aid, or blessed his hand."

Tickell, in his "Prospect of Peace," has the same hope of a new academy:-

"In happy chains our daring language bound, Shall sport no more in arbitrary sound."

Whether the similitude of those passages, which exhibit the same thought on the same occasion, proceeded from accident or imitation, is not easy to determine. Tickell might have been impressed with his expectation by Swift's "Proposal for Ascertaining the English Language," then lately published.

In the Parliament that met in 1701 he was chosen representative of East Grinstead. Perhaps it was about this time that he changed his party, for he voted for the impeachment of those lords who had persuaded the king to the Partition Treaty, a treaty in which he himself had been ministerially employed.

A great part of Queen Anne's reign was a time of war, in which there was little employment for negotiators, and Prior had, therefore, leisure to make or to polish verses. When the Battle of Blenheim called forth all the verse-men, Prior, among the rest, took care to show his delight in the increasing honour of his country by an epistle to Boileau. He published, soon afterwards, a volume of poems, with the encomiastic character of his deceased patron, the Earl of Dorset. It began with the College exercise, and ended with the "Nutbrown Maid."

The Battle of Ramillies soon afterwards (in 1706) excited him to another effort of poetry. On this occasion he had fewer or less formidable rivals, and it would be not easy to name any other composition produced by that event which is now remembered.

Everything has its day. Through the reigns of William and Anne no prosperous event passed undignified by poetry. In the last war, when France was disgraced and overpowered in every quarter of the globe, when Spain, coming to her assistance, only shared her calamities, and the name of an Englishman was reverenced through Europe, no poet was heard amidst the general acclamation; the fame of our counsellors and heroes was entrusted to the Gazetteer. The nation in time grew weary of the war, and the queen grew weary of her ministers. The war was burdensome, and the ministers were insolent. Harley and his friends began to hope that they might, by driving the Whigs from court and from power, gratify at once the queen and the people. There was now a call for writers, who might convey intelligence of past abuses, and show the waste of public money, the unreasonable conduct of the allies, the avarice of generals, the tyranny of minions, and the general danger of approaching ruin. For this purpose a paper called the Examiner was periodically published, written, as it happened, by any wit of the party, and sometimes, as is said, by Mrs. Manley. Some are owned by Swift; and one, in ridicule of Garth's verses to Godolphin upon the loss of his place, was written by Prior, and answered by Addison, who appears to have known the author either by conjecture or intelligence.

The Tories, who were now in power, were in haste to end the war, and Prior, being recalled (1710) to his former employment of making treaties, was sent (July, 1711) privately to Paris with propositions of peace. He was remembered at the French court; and, returning in about a month, brought with him the Abbe Gaultier and M. Mesnager, a minister from France, invested with full powers. This transaction not being avowed, Mackay, the master of the Dover packet-boat, either zealously or officiously, seized Prior and his associates at Canterbury. It is easily supposed they were soon released.

The negotiation was begun at Prior's house, where the queen's ministers met Mesnager (September 20, 1711), and entered privately upon the great business. The importance of Prior appears from the mention made of him by St. John in his letter to the queen:-

"My Lord Treasurer moved, and all my Lords were of the same opinion, that Mr. Prior should be added to those who are empowered to sign; the reason for which is because he, having personally treated with Monsieur de Torcy, is the best witness we can produce of the sense in which the general preliminary engagements are entered into; besides which, as he is the best versed in matters of trade of all your Majesty's servants who have been trusted in this secret, if you shall think fit to employ him in the future treaty of commerce, it will be of consequence that he has been a party concerned in concluding that convention, which must be the rule of this treaty."

The assembly of this important night was in some degree clandestine, the design of treaty not being yet openly declared and when the Whigs returned to power was aggravated to a charge of high treason; though, as Prior remarks in his imperfect answer to the Report of the Committee of Secrecy, no treaty ever was made without private interviews and preliminary discussions.

My business is not the history of the peace, but the life of Prior. The conferences began at Utrecht on the 1st of January (1711-12), and the English plenipotentiaries arrived on the 15th. The ministers of the different potentates conferred and conferred; but the peace advanced so slowly that speedier methods were found necessary, and Bolingbroke was sent to Paris to adjust differences with less formality. Prior either accompanied him or followed him, and after his departure had the appointments and authority of an ambassador, though no public character. By some mistake of the queen's orders the court of France had been disgusted, and Bolingbroke says in his letter, "Dear Mat,--Hide the nakedness of thy country, and give the best turn thy fertile brain will furnish thee with to the blunders of thy countrymen, who are not much better politicians than the French are poets."

Soon after, the Duke of Shrewsbury went on a formal embassy to Paris. It is related by Boyer that the intention was to have joined Prior in the commission, but that Shrewsbury refused to be associated with a man so meanly born. Prior therefore continued to act without a title till the duke returned next year to England, and then he assumed the style and dignity of ambassador. But while he continued in appearance a private man, he was treated with confidence by Louis, who sent him with a letter to the queen, written in favour of the Elector of Bavaria. "I shall expect," says he, "with impatience, the return of Mr. Prior, whose conduct is very agreeable to me." And while the Duke of Shrewsbury was still at Paris, Bolingbroke wrote to Prior thus:- "Monsieur de Torcy has a confidence in you; make use of it, once for all, upon this occasion, and convince him thoroughly that we must give a different turn to our Parliament and our people according to their resolution at this crisis."

Prior's public dignity and splendour commenced in August, 1713, and continued till the August following; but I am afraid that, according to the usual fate of greatness, it was attended with some perplexities and mortifications. He had not all that is customarily given to ambassadors: he hints to the queen in an imperfect poem that he had no service of plate; and it appeared by the debts which he contracted that his remittances were not punctually made.

On the 1st of August, 1714, ensued the downfall of the Tories and the degradation of Prior. He was recalled, but was not able to return, being detained by the debts which he had found it necessary to contract, and which were not discharged before March, though his old friend Montague was now at the head of the Treasury. He returned, then, as soon as he could, and was welcomed on the 25th of March by a warrant, but was, however, suffered to live in his own house, under the custody of the messenger, till he was examined before a committee of the Privy Council, of which Mr. Walpole was chairman, and Lord Coningsby, Mr. Stanhope, and Mr.

Lechmere were the principal interrogators, who, in this examination, of which there is printed an account not unentertaining, behaved with the boisterousness of men elated by recent authority. They are represented as asking questions sometimes vague, sometimes insidious, and writing answers different from those which they received. Prior, however, seems to have been overpowered by their turbulence; for he confesses that he signed what, if he had ever come before a legal judicature, he should have contradicted or explained away. The oath was administered by Boscawen, a Middlesex justice, who at last was going to write his attestation on the wrong side of the paper. They were very industrious to find some charge against Oxford, and asked Prior, with great earnestness, who was present when the preliminary articles were talked of or signed at his house? He told them that either the Earl of Oxford or the Duke of Shrewsbury was absent, but he could not remember which, an answer which perplexed them, because it supplied no accusation against either. "Could anything be more absurd," says he, "or more inhuman, than to propose to me a question, by the answering of which I might, according to them, prove myself a traitor? And notwithstanding their solemn promise that nothing which I should say should hurt myself, I had no reason to trust them, for they violated that promise about five hours after. However, I owned I was there present. Whether this was wisely done or no I leave to my friends to determine." When he had signed the paper, he was told by Walpole that the committee were not satisfied with his behaviour, nor could give such an account of it to the Commons as might merit favour; and that they now thought a stricter confinement necessary than to his own house. "Here," says he, "Boscawen played the moralist, and Coningsby the Christian, but both very awkwardly." The messenger, in whose custody he was to be placed, was then called, and very indecently asked by Coningsby "if his house was secured by bars and bolts." The messenger answered, "No," with astonishment. At which Coningsby very angrily said, "Sir, you must secure this prisoner; it is for the safety of the nation: if he escape, you shall answer for it."

They had already printed their report; and in this examination were endeavouring to find proofs.

He continued thus confined for some time; and Mr. Walpole (June 10, 1715) moved for an impeachment against him. What made him so acrimonious does not appear; he was by nature no thirster for blood. Prior was a week after committed to close custody, with orders that "no person should be admitted to see him without leave from the Speaker." When, two years after, an Act of Grace was passed, he was excepted, and continued still in custody, which he had made less tedious by writing his "Alma." He was, however, soon after discharged. He had now his liberty, but he had nothing else. Whatever the profit of his employments might have been, he had always spent it; and at the age of fifty-three was, with all his abilities, in danger of penury, having yet no solid revenue but from the fellowship of his college, which, when in his exaltation he was censured for retaining it, he said he could live upon at last. Being, however, generally known and esteemed, he was encouraged to add other poems to those which he had printed, and to publish them by subscription. The expedient succeeded by the industry of many friends, who circulated the proposals, and the care of some who, it is said, withheld the money from him lest he should squander it. The price of the volume was two guineas; the whole collection was four thousand; to which Lord Harley, the son of the Earl of Oxford, to whom he had invariably adhered, added an equal sum for the purchase of Down Hall, which Prior was to enjoy during life, and Harley after his decease. He had now, what wits and philosophers have often wished, the power of passing the day in contemplative tranquillity. But it seems that busy men seldom live long in a state of quiet. It is not unlikely that his health declined, he complains of deafness; "for," says he, "I took little care of my ears while I was not sure if my head was my own."

Of any occurrences of his remaining life I have found no account. In a letter to Swift, "I have," says he, "treated Lady Harriet, at Cambridge (a Fellow of a College treat!) and spoke verses to her in a gown and cap! What, the plenipotentiary, so far concerned in the damned peace at Utrecht; the man that makes up half the volume of terse prose, that makes up the report of the committee, speaking verses! Sic est, homo sum."

He died at Wimpole, a seat of the Earl of Oxford, on the 18th of September, 1721, and was buried in Westminster; where on a monument, for which, as the "last piece of human vanity," he left five hundred pounds, is engraven this epitaph:-

Sui Temporis Historiam meditanti, Paulatim obrepens Febris Operi simul et Vitae filum abrupit, Sept. 18. An. Dom. 1721. AEtat. 57. H.S.E. Vir Eximius Serenissimis Regi GULIELMO Reginaeque MARIAE In Congressione Foederatorum Hagae anno 1690 celebrata, Deinde Magnae Britanniae Legatis Tum iis, Qui anno

1697 Pacem RYSWICKI confecerunt, Tum iis, Qui apud Gallos annie proximis Legationem obierunt Eodem etiani anno 1657 in Hibernia SECRETARIUS; Necnon in utroque Honorabili consessu Eorum, Qui anno 1700 ordinandis Commercii negotiis, Quique anno 1711 dirigendis Portorii rebus, Praeidebant, COMMISSIONARIUS; Postremo ab ANNA, Felicissimae memoriae Regina, Ad LUDOVICUM XIV. Galliae Regem Missus anno 1711 De Pace stabilienda (Pace etiam num durante Diuque ut boni jam omnes sperant duratura), Cum sunma potestate Legatus; MATTHAES PRIOR Armiger Qui Hos omnes, quibus cumulates est, Titulos Humanitatis, Ingenii, Ereditionis laude Superavit; Cui enim nascenti faciles arriserant Mesae. Hunc Puerum Schola hic Regia perpolivit; Jevenem in Collegio S'ti Johannis Cantabrigia optimis Scientiis instruxit; Virum denique auxit, et perfecit, Multa cum viris Principibus censuetudo; Ita natus, ita institutus, A Vatam Choro avelli numquam potuit, Sed solebat saepe rerum civilium gravitatem Amoeniorum Literarum Studiis condire: Et cum omne adeo Poetices genus Haud infeliciter tentaret, Tum in Fabellis concinne lepideque texendis Mirus Artifex Neminem habuit parem. Haec liberalis animi oblectamenta: Quam nullo illi labore constiterint, Facile ii perspexere, quibus usus est Amici; Apud quos Urbanitatem et Leporum plenus Cum ad rem, quaecunque forte inciderat, Apte varie copioseque alluderet, Interea nihil quaesitum, nihil vi expressum Videbatur, Sed omnia ultro effluere, Et quasi jugi e foote affatim exuberare, Ita suos tandem dubios reliquit, Essetne in Scriptis, Poeta Elegantior, An in Convictu, Comes Jocundior.

Of Prior, eminent as he was, both by his abilities and station, very few memorials have been left by his contemporaries; the account, therefore, must now be destitute of his private character and familiar practices. He lived at a time when the rage of party detected all which it was any man's interest to hide; and, as little ill is heard of Prior, it is certain that not much was known. He was not afraid of provoking censure; for when he forsook the Whigs, under whose patronage he first entered the world, he became a Tory so ardent and determinate. that he did not willingly consort with men of different opinions. He was one of the sixteen Tories who met weekly, and agreed to address each other by the title of Brother; and seems to have adhered, not only by concurrence of political designs, but by peculiar affection, to the Earl of Oxford and his family. With how much confidence he was trusted has been already told.

He was, however, in Pope's opinion, fit only to make verses, and less qualified for business than Addison himself. This was surely said without consideration. Addison, exalted to a high place, was forced into degradation by the sense of his own incapacity; Prior, who was employed by men very capable of estimating his value, having been secretary to one embassy, had, when great abilities were again wanted, the same office another time; and was, after so much experience of his own knowledge and dexterity, at last sent to transact a negotiation in the highest degree arduous and important, for which he was qualified, among other requisites, in the opinion of Bolingbroke, by his influence upon the French minister, and by skill in questions of commerce above other men.

Of his behaviour in the lighter parts of life, it is too late to get much intelligence. One of his answers to a boastful Frenchman has been related; and to an impertinent he made another equally proper. During his embassy he sat at the opera by a man who, in his rapture, accompanied with his own voice the principal singer.

Prior fell to railing at the performer with all the terms of reproach that he could collect, till the Frenchman, ceasing from his song, began to expostulate with him for his harsh censure of a man who was confessedly the ornament of the stage. "I know all that," says the ambassador, "mais il chante si haut, que je ne scaurois vous entendre."

In a gay French company, where every one sang a little song or stanza, of which the burden was "Bannissons la Melancolie," when it came to his turn to sing, after the performance of a young lady that sat next him, he produced these extemporary lines

"Mais cette voix, et ces beaux yeux, Font Cupidon trop dangereux, Et je suis triste quand je crie Bannissons la Melancolie."

Tradition represents him as willing to descend from the dignity of the poet and statesman to the low delights of mean company. His Chloe probably was sometimes ideal: but the woman with whom he cohabited was a despicable drab of the lowest species. One of his wenches, perhaps Chloe, while he was absent from his house, stole his plate and ran away, as was related by a woman who had been his servant. Of his propensity to sordid converse, I have seen an account so seriously ridiculous, that it seems to deserve insertion.

"I have been assured that Prior, after having spent the evening with Oxford,

Bolingbroke, Pope, and Swift, would go and smoke a pipe and drink a bottle of ale with a common soldier and his wife in Long Acre before he went to bed, not from any remains of the lowness of his original, as one said, but I suppose that his faculties -

"'--strained to the height, In that celestial colloquy sublime, Dazzled and spent, sunk down, and sought repair.'"

Poor Prior; why was he so STRAINED, and in such WANT OF REPAIR, after a conversation with men not, in the opinion of the world, much wiser than himself? But such are the conceits of speculatists, who STRAIN their FACULTIES to find in a mine what lies upon the surface. His opinions, so far as the means of judging are left us, seem to have been right; but his life was, it seems, irregular, negligent, and sensual.

Prior has written with great variety, and his variety has made him popular. He has tried all styles, from the grotesque to the solemn, and has not so failed in any as to incur derision or disgrace. His works may be distinctly considered as comprising Tales, Love Verses, Occasional Poems, "Alma," and "Solomon."

His tales have obtained general approbation, being written with great familiarity and great sprightliness; the language is easy, but seldom gross, and the numbers smooth, without appearance of care. Of these tales there are only four: "The Ladle," which is introduced by a preface, neither necessary nor pleasing, neither grave nor merry. "Paulo Purganti," which has likewise a preface, but of more value than the tale. "Hans Carvel," not over-decent; and "Protogenes and Apelles," an old story mingled, by an affectation not disagreeable, with modern images. "The Young Gentleman in Love" has hardly a just claim to the title of a tale. I know not whether he be the original author of any tale which he has given us. The adventure of Hans Carvel has passed through many successions of merry wits, for it is to be found in Ariosto's "Satires," and is perhaps yet older. But the merit of such stories is the art of telling them.

In his amorous effusions he is less happy; for they are not dictated by nature or by passion, and have neither gallantry nor tenderness. They have the coldness of Cowley, without his wit, the dull exercises of a skilful versifier, resolved at all adventures to write something about Chloe, and trying to be amorous by dint of study. His fictions, therefore, are mythological. Venus, after the example of the

Greek epigram, asks when she was seen NAKED AND BATHING. Then Cupid is MISTAKEN; then Cupid is DISARMED; then he loses his darts to Ganymede; then Jupiter sends him a summons by Mercury. Then Chloe goes a-hunting with an IVORY QUIVER GRACEFUL AT HER SIDE; Diana mistakes her for one of her nymphs, and Cupid laughs at the blunder. All this is surely despicable; and even when he tries to act the lover without the help of gods or goddesses, his thoughts are unaffecting or remote. He talks not "like a man of this world."

The greatest of all his amorous essays is "Henry and Emma," a dull and tedious dialogue, which excites neither esteem for the man nor tenderness for the woman. The example of Emma, who resolves to follow an outlawed murderer wherever fear and guilt shall drive him, deserves no imitation; and the experiment by which Henry tries the lady's constancy is such as must end either in infamy to her or in disappointment to himself.

His occasional poems necessarily lost part of their value, as their occasions, being less remembered, raised less emotion, Some of them, however, are preserved by their inherent excellence. The burlesque of Boileau's ode on Namur has in some parts such airiness and levity as will always procure it readers, even among those who cannot compare it with the original. The epistle to Boileau is not so happy. The "Poems to the King," are now perused only by young students, who read merely that they may learn to write; and of the "Carmen Seculare," I cannot but suspect that I might praise or censure it by caprice without danger of detection; for who can be supposed to have laboured through it? Yet the time has been when this neglected work was so popular that it was translated into Latin by no common master.

His poem on the Battle of Ramillies is necessarily tedious by the form of the stanza. An uniform mass of ten lines thirty-five times repeated, inconsequential and slightly connected, must weary both the ear and the understanding. His imitation of Spenser, which consists principally in *I* WEEN and *I* WEET, without exclusion of later modes of speech, makes his poem neither ancient nor modern. His mention of Mars and Bellona, and his comparison of Marlborough to the eagle that bears the thunder of Jupiter, are all puerile and unaffecting; and yet more despicable is the long tale told by Louis in his despair of Brute and Troynovante, and the teeth of Cadmus, with his similes of the raven and eagle and wolf and lion. By the help of such easy fictions and vulgar topics, without acquaintance with life, and without knowledge of art or nature, a poem of any length, cold and lifeless like this, may be easily written on any subject.

In his epilogues to Phaedra and to Lucius he is very happily facetious; but in the prologue before the queen the pedant has found his way with Minerva, Perseus, and Andromeda.

His epigrams and lighter pieces are, like those of others, sometimes elegant, sometimes trifling, and sometimes dull; among the best are the "Chamelion" and the epitaph on John and Joan.

Scarcely any one of our poets has written so much and translated so little: the version of Callimachus is sufficiently licentious; the paraphrase on St. Paul's Exhortation to Charity is eminently beautiful.

"Alma" is written in professed imitation of "Hudibras," and has at least one accidental resemblance: "Hudibras" wants a plan because it is left imperfect; "Alma" is imperfect because it seems never to have had a plan. Prior appears not to have proposed to himself any drift or design, but to have written the casual dictates of the present moment.

What Horace said when he imitated Lucilius, might be said of Butler by Prior; his numbers were not smooth nor neat. Prior excelled him in versification; but he was, like Horace, inventore minor; he had not Butler's exuberance of matter and variety of illustration. The spangles of wit which he could afford he knew how to polish; but he wanted the bullion of his master. Butler pours out a negligent profusion, certain of the weight, but careless of the stamp. Prior has comparatively little, but with that little he makes a fine show. "Alma" has many admirers, and was the only piece among Prior's works of which Pope said that he should wish to be the author.

"Solomon" is the work to which he entrusted the protection of his name, and which he expected succeeding ages to regard with veneration. His affection was natural; it had undoubtedly been written with great labour; and who is willing to think that he has been labouring in vain? He had infused into it much knowledge and much thought; had often polished it to elegance, often dignified it with splendour, and sometimes heightened it to sublimity: he perceived in it many excellences, and did not discover that it wanted that without which all others are of small avail--the power of engaging attention and alluring curiosity.

Tediousness is the most fatal of all faults; negligence or errors are single and local, but tediousness pervades the whole; other faults are censured and forgotten, but the power of tediousness propagates itself. He that is weary the first hour is more weary the second, as bodies forced into motion, contrary to their tendency, pass more and more slowly through every successive interval of space. Unhappily this pernicious failure is that which an author is least able to discover. We are seldom tiresome to ourselves; and the act of composition fills and delights the mind with change of language and succession of images. Every couplet, when produced, is new, and novelty is the great source of pleasure. Perhaps no man ever thought a line superfluous when he first wrote it, or contracted his work till his ebullitions of invention had subsided. And even if he should control his desire of immediate renown, and keep his work NINE YEARS unpublished, he will be still the author, and still in danger of deceiving himself: and if he consults his friends he will probably find men who have more kindness than judgment, or more fear to offend than desire to instruct. The tediousness of this poem proceeds not from the uniformity of the subject, for it is sufficiently diversified, but from the continued tenor of the narration; in which Solomon relates the successive vicissitudes of his own mind without the intervention of any other speaker or the mention of any other agent, unless it be Abra; the reader is only to learn what he thought, and to be told that he thought wrong. The event of every experiment is foreseen, and therefore the process is not much regarded. Yet the work is far from deserving to be neglected. He that shall peruse it will be able to mark many passages to which he may recur for instruction or delight; many from which the poet may learn to write and the philosopher to reason.

If Prior's poetry be generally considered, his praise will be that of correctness and industry, rather than of compass of comprehension or activity of fancy. He never made any effort of invention: his greater pieces are only tissues of common thoughts; and his smaller, which consist of light images or single conceits, are not always his own. I have traced him among the French epigrammatists, and have been informed that he poached for prey among obscure authors. The "Thief and Cordelier" is, I suppose, generally considered as an original production, with how much justice this epigram may tell, which was written by Georgius Sabinus, a poet now little known or read, though once the friend of Luther and Melancthon:-

"De Sacerdote Furem consolante. "Quidam sacrificus furem comitatus euntem Huc ubi dat sontes carnificina neci. Ne sis moestus, ait; summi conviva Tonantis Jam cum coelitibus (si modo credis) eris. Ille gemens, si vera mihi solatia praebes, Hospes apud superos sis meus oro, refert. Sacrificus contra; mihi non convivia fas est Ducere, jejunas hac edo luce nihil."

What he has valuable he owes to his diligence and his judgment. His diligence has justly placed him amongst the most correct of the English poets; and he was one of the first that resolutely endeavoured at correctness. He never sacrifices accuracy to haste, nor indulges himself in contemptuous negligence, or impatient idleness; he has no careless lines, or entangled sentiments; his words are nicely selected, and his thoughts fully expanded. If this part of his character suffers an abatement, it must be from the disproportion of his rhymes, which have not always sufficient consonance, and from the admission of broken lines into his "Solomon;" but perhaps he thought, like Cowley, that hemistichs ought to be admitted into heroic poetry.

He had apparently such rectitude of judgment as secured him from everything that approached to the ridiculous or absurd; but as law operates in civil agency, not to the excitement of virtue, but the repression of wickedness, so judgment in the operations of intellect can hinder faults, but not produce excellence. Prior is never low, nor very often sublime. It is said by Longinus of Euripides, that he forces himself sometimes into grandeur by violence of effort, as the lion kindles his fury by the lashes of his own tail. Whatever Prior obtains above mediocrity seems the effort of struggle and of toil. He has many vigorous, but few happy lines; he has everything by purchase, and nothing by gift; he had no NIGHTLY VISITATIONS of the Muse, no infusions of sentiment or felicities of fancy. His diction, however, is more his own than of any among the successors of Dryden; he borrows no lucky turns, or commodious modes of language, from his predecessors. His phrases are original, but they are sometimes harsh; as he inherited no elegances, none has he bequeathed. His expression has every mark of laborious study, the line seldom seems to have been formed at once; the words did not come till they were called, and were then put by constraint into their places, where they do their duty, but do it sullenly. In his greater compositions there may be found more rigid stateliness than graceful dignity.

Of versification he was not negligent. What he received from Dryden he did not lose; neither did he increase the difficulty of writing by unnecessary severity, but uses triplets and alexandrines without scruple. In his preface to "Solomon" he proposes some improvements by extending the sense from one couplet to another with variety of pauses. This he has attempted, but without success; his interrupted lines are unpleasing, and his sense, as less distinct, is less striking. He has altered the stanza of Spenser as a house is altered by building another in its place of a different form. With how little resemblance he has formed his new stanza to that of his master these specimens will show:-

SPENSER.

"She flying fast from Heaven's fated face, And from the world that her discovered wide, Fled to the wasteful wilderness space, From living eyes her open shame to hide, And lurked in rocks and caves long unespied. But that fair crew of knights, and Una fair, Did in that castle afterwards abide, To rest themselves, and weary powers repair, Where store they found of all that dainty was and rare?"

PRIOR.

"To the close rock the frightened raven flies, Soon as the rising eagle cuts the air; The shaggy wolf unseen and trembling lies, When the hoarse roar proclaims the lion near. Ill-starred did we our forts and lines forsake, To dare our British foes to open fight: Our conquest we by stratagem should make; Our triumph had been founded in our flight. 'Tis ours by craft and by surprise to gain; 'Tis theirs to meet in arms, and battle in the plain."

By this new structure of his lines he has avoided difficulties; nor am I sure that he has lost any of the power of pleasing, but he no longer imitates Spencer. Some of his poems are written without regularity of measures; for, when he commenced poet, he had not recovered from our Pindaric infatuation; but he probably lived to be convinced that the essence of verse is order and consonance. His numbers are such as mere diligence may attain; they seldom offend the ear, and seldom soothe it; they commonly want airiness, lightness, and facility. What is smooth is not soft. His verses always roll, but they seldom flow.

A survey of the life and writings of Prior may exemplify a sentence which he doubtless understood well when he read Horace at his uncle's, "The vessel long retains the scent which it first receives." In his private relaxation he revived the tavern, and in his amorous pedantry he exhibited the college. But on higher occasions and nobler subjects, when habit was overpowered by the necessity of reflection, he wanted not wisdom as a statesman, or elegance as a poet.

CONGREVE

William Congreve descended from a family in Staffordshire of so great antiquity, that it claims a place among the few that extend their hue beyond the Norman Conquest, and was the son of William Congreve, second son of Richard Congreve, of Congreve and Stratton. He visited, once at least, the residence of his ancestors; and, I believe, more places than one are still shown in groves and gardens, where he is related to have written his Old Bachelor.

Neither the time nor place of his birth is certainly known. If the inscription upon his monument be true, he was born in 1672. For the place, it was said by himself that he owed his nativity to England, and by everybody else that he was born in Ireland. Southern mentioned him with sharp censure as a man that meanly disowned his native country. The biographers assigned his nativity to Bardsa, near Leeds, in Yorkshire, from the account given by himself, as they suppose, to Jacob. To doubt whether a man of eminence has told the truth about his own birth is, in appearance, to be very deficient in candour; yet nobody can live long without knowing that falsehoods of convenience or vanity, falsehoods from which no evil immediately visible ensues, except the general degradation of human testimony, are very lightly uttered, and once uttered are sullenly supported. Boileau, who desired to be thought a rigorous and steady moralist, having told a pretty lie to Louis XIV., continued it afterwards by false dates; thinking himself obliged IN HONOUR, says his admirer, to maintain what, when he said it, was so well received. [Congreve was baptised at Bardsey, February 10, 1670.]

Wherever Congreve was born, he was educated first at Kilkenny, and afterwards at Dublin, his father having some military employment that stationed him in Ireland; but after having passed through the usual preparatory studies, as may be reasonably supposed, with great celerity and success, his father thought it proper to assign him a profession, by which something might be gotten, and about the time of the Revolution sent him, at the age of sixteen, to study law in the Middle Temple, where he lived for several years, but with very little attention to statutes or reports. His disposition to become an author appeared very early, as he very early felt that force of imagination, and possessed that copiousness of sentiment, by which intellectual pleasure can be given. His first performance was a novel called "Incognita; or, Love and Duty Reconciled;" it is praised by the biographers, who quote some part of the preface, that is, indeed, for such a time of life, uncommonly judicious. I would rather praise it than read it.

His first dramatic labour was The Old Bachelor, of which he says, in his defence against Collier, "That comedy was written, as several know, some years before it was acted. When I wrote it I had little thoughts of the stage; but did it to amuse myself in a slow recovery from a fit of sickness. Afterwards, through my indiscretion it was seen, and in some little time more it was acted; and I, through the remainder of my indiscretion suffered myself to be drawn into the prosecution of a difficult and thankless study, and to be involved in a perpetual war with knaves and fools."

There seems to be a strange affectation in authors of appearing to have done everything by chance. The Old Bachelor was written for amusement in the languor of convalescence. Yet it is apparently composed with great elaborateness of dialogue, and incessant ambition of wit. The age of the writer considered, it is indeed a very wonderful performance; for, whenever written, it was acted (1693) when he was not more than twenty-one years old; and was then recommended by Mr. Dryden, Mr. Southern, and Mr. Maynwaring. Dryden said that he never had seen such a first play; but they found it deficient in some things necessary to the success of its exhibition, and by their greater experience fitted it for the stage. Southern used to relate of one comedy, probably of this, that when Congreve read it to the players he pronounced it so wretchedly, that they had almost rejected it; but they were afterwards so well persuaded of its excellence that, for half a year before it was acted, the manager allowed its author the privilege of the house.

Few plays have ever been so beneficial to the writer, for it procured him the patronage of Halifax, who immediately made him one of the commissioners for licensing coaches, and soon after gave him a place in the Pipe-office, and another in the Customs, of six hundred pounds a year. Congreve's conversation must surely have been at least equally pleasing with his writings.

Such a comedy, written at such an age, requires some consideration. As the lighter species of dramatic poetry professes the imitation of common life, of real manners. and daily incidents, it apparently presupposes a familiar knowledge of many characters, and exact observation of the passing world; the difficulty, therefore, is to conceive how this knowledge can be obtained by a boy.

But if The Old Bachelor be more nearly examined, it will be found to be one of those comedies which may be made by a mind vigorous and acute, and furnished with comic characters by the perusal of other poets, without much actual commerce with mankind. The dialogue is one constant reciprocation of conceits or clash of wit, in which nothing flows necessarily from the occasion, or is dictated by nature. The characters, both of men and women, are either fictitious and artificial, as those of Heartwell and the ladies, or easy and common, as Wittol, a tame idiot; Bluff, a swaggering coward; and Fondlewife, a jealous Puritan; and the catastrophe arises from a mistake, not very probably produced, by marrying a woman in a mask. Yet this gay comedy, when all these deductions are made, will still remain the work of very powerful and fertile faculties; the dialogue is quick and sparkling, the incidents such as seize the attention, and the wit so exuberant that it "o'er- informs its tenement."

Next year he gave another specimen of his abilities in The Double Dealer, which was not received with equal kindness. He writes to his patron the Lord Halifax a dedication, in which he endeavours to reconcile the reader to that which found few friends among the audience. These apologies are always useless: de gestibus non est disputandem. Men may be convinced, but they cannot be pleased, against their will. But though taste is obstinate, it is very variable, and time often prevails when arguments have failed. Queen Mary conferred upon both those plays the honour of her presence; and when she died soon after, Congreve testified his gratitude by a despicable effusion of elegiac pastoral, a composition in which all is unnatural and yet nothing is new.

In another year (1695) his prolific pen produced Love for Love, a comedy of nearer alliance to life, and exhibiting more real manners, than either of the former. The character of Foresight was then common. Dryden calculated nativities; both Cromwell and King William had their lucky days; and Shaftesbury himself, though he had no religion, was said to regard predictions. The Sailor is not accounted very natural, but he is very pleasant. With this play was opened the New Theatre, under the direction of Betterton, the tragedian, where he exhibited two years afterwards (1687) The Mourning Bride, a tragedy, so written as to show him sufficiently qualified for either kind of dramatic poetry. In this play, of which, when he afterwards revised it, he reduced the versification to greater regularity; there is more bustle than sentiment; the plot is busy and intricate, and the events take hold on the attention; but, except a very few passages, we are rather amused with noise and perplexed with stratagem, than entertained with any true delineation of natural characters. This, however, was received with more benevolence than any other of his works, and still continues to be acted and applauded.

But whatever objections may be made either to his comic or tragic excellence, they are lost at once in the blaze of admiration, when it is remembered that he had produced these four plays before he had passed his twenty-fifth year, before other men, even such as are some time to shine in eminence, have passed their probation of literature, or presume to hope for any other notice than such as is bestowed on diligence and inquiry. Among all the efforts of early genius, which literary history records, I doubt whether any one can be produced that more surpasses the common limits of nature than the plays of Congreve.

About this time began the long-continued controversy between Collier and the poets. In the reign of Charles I. the Puritans had raised a violent clamour against the drama, which they considered as an entertainment not lawful to Christians, an opinion held by them in common with the Church of Rome; and Prynne published "Histriomastix," a huge volume in which stage-plays were censured. The outrages and crimes of the Puritans brought afterwards their whole system of doctrine into disrepute, and from the Restoration the poets and players were left at quiet; for to have molested them would have had the appearance of tendency to puritanical malignity. This danger, however, was worn away by time, and Collier, a fierce and implacable non-juror, knew that an attack upon the theatre would never make him suspected for a Puritan; he therefore (1698) published "A Short View of the Immorality and Profaneness of the English Stage," I believe with no other motive than religious zeal and honest indignation. He was formed for a controvertist, with sufficient learning, with diction vehement and pointed, though often vulgar and incorrect, with unconquerable pertinacity, with wit in the highest degree and sarcastic, and with all those powers exalted and invigorated by just confidence in his cause. Thus qualified and thus incited, he walked out to battle, and assailed at once most of the living writers, from Dryden to Durfey. His onset was violent; those passages, which, while they stood single, had passed with little notice, when they were accumulated and exposed together, excited horror. The wise and the pious caught the alarm, and the nation wondered why it had so long suffered irreligion and licentiousness to be openly taught at the public charge.

Nothing now remained for the poets but to resist or fly. Dryden's conscience or his prudence, angry as he was, withheld him from the conflict. Congreve and Vanbrugh attempted answers. Congreve, a very young man, elated with success, and impatient of censure, assumed an air of confidence and security. His chief art of controversy is to retort upon his adversary his own words: he is very angry, and hoping to conquer Collier with his own weapons, allows himself in the use of every term of contumely and contempt, but he has the sword without the arm of Scanderbeg; he has his antagonist's coarseness but not his strength. Collier replied, for contest was his delight. "He was not to be frighted from his purpose or his prey."

The cause of Congreve was not tenable; whatever glosses he might use for the defence or palliation of single passages, the general tenour and tendency of his plays must always be condemned. It is acknowledged, with universal conviction, that the perusal of his works will make no man better, and that their ultimate effect is to represent pleasure in alliance with vice, and to relax those obligations by which life ought to be regulated.

The stage found other advocates, and the dispute was protracted through ten years: but at last comedy grew more modest, and Collier lived to see the reformation of the theatre.

Of the powers by which this important victory was achieved, a quotation from Love for Love, and the remark upon it, may afford a specimen:-

Sir Samps. "Sampson's a very good name; for your Sampsons were strong dogs from the beginning."

Angel. "Have a care--if you remember, the strongest Sampson of your name pulled an old house over his head at last."

"Here you have the sacred history burlesqued, and Sampson once more brought into the house of Dagon, to make sport for the Philistines!"

Congreve's last play was The Way of The World, which, though, as he hints in him dedication it was written with great labour and much thought, was received with so little favour, that being in a high degree offended and disgusted, he resolved to commit his quiet and his fame no more to the caprices of an audience.

From this time his life ceased to be public; he lived for himself and his friends, and among his friends was able to name every man of his time whom wit and elegance had raised to reputation. It may be therefore reasonably supposed that his manners were polite, and his conversation pleasing. He seems not to have taken much pleasure in writing, as he contributed nothing to the Spectator, and only one paper to the Tatler, though published by men with whom he might be supposed willing to associate: and though he lived many years after the publication of his "Miscellaneous Poems," yet he added nothing to them, but lived on in literary indolence, engaged in no controversy, contending with no rival, neither soliciting flattery by public commendations, nor provoking enmity by malignant criticism, but passing his time among the great and splendid, in the placid enjoyment of his fame and fortune.

Having owed his fortune to Halifax, he continued, always of his patron's party, but, as it seems, without violence or acrimony, and his firmness was naturally esteemed, as his abilities were reverenced. His security therefore was never violated; and when, upon the extrusion of the Whigs, some intercession was used lest Congreve should be displaced, the Earl of Oxford made this answer:-

"Non obtusa adeo gestamus pectora Poeni, Nec tam aversus equos Tyria sol jungit ab urbe."

He that was thus honoured by the adverse party might naturally expect to be advanced when his friends returned to power, and he was accordingly made secretary for the island of Jamaica, a place, I suppose without trust or care, but which, with his post in the Customs, is said to have afforded him twelve hundred pounds a year. His honours were yet far greater than his profits. Every writer mentioned him with respect, and among other testimonies to his merit, Steele made him the patron of his "Miscellany," and Pope inscribed to him his translations of the "Iliad." But he treated the muses with ingratitude; for, having long conversed familiarly with the great, he wished to be considered rather as a man of fashion than of wit; and, when he received a visit from Voltaire, disgusted him by the despicable foppery of desiring to be considered not as an author but a gentleman; to which the Frenchman replied, "that, if he had been only a gentleman, he should not have come to visit him."

In his retirement he may be supposed to have applied himself to books, for he discovers more literature than the poets have commonly attained. But his studies were in his later days obstructed by cataracts in his eyes, which at last terminated in blindness. This melancholy state was aggravated by the gout, for which he sought relief by a journey to Bath: but, being overturned in his chariot, complained from that time of a pain in his side, and died at his house in Surrey Street in the Strand, January 29, 1728-9. Having lain in state in the Jerusalem Chamber, he was buried in Westminster Abbey, where a monument is erected to his memory by Henrietta Duchess of Marlborough, to whom, for reasons either not known or not mentioned, he bequeathed a legacy of about ten thousand pounds, the accumulation of attentive parsimony, which, though to her superfluous and useless, might have given great assistance to the ancient family from which he descended, at that time, by the imprudence of his relation, reduced to difficulties and distress.

Congreve has merit of the highest kind; he is an original writer, who borrowed neither the models of his plot nor the manner of his dialogue. Of his plays I cannot speak distinctly, for since I inspected them many years have passed, but what remains upon my memory is, that his characters are commonly fictitious and artificial, with very little of nature, and not much of life. He formed a peculiar idea of comic excellence, which he supposed to consist in gay remarks and unexpected answers; but that which he endeavoured, he seldom failed of performing. His scenes exhibit not much of humour, imagery, or passion: his personages are a kind of intellectual gladiators; every sentence is to ward or strike; the contest of smartness is never intermitted; his wit is a meteor playing to and fro with alternate coruscations. His comedies have, therefore, in some degree, the operation of tragedies, they surprise rather than divert, and raise admiration oftener than merriment. But they are the works of a mind replete with images, and quick in combination.

Of his miscellaneous poetry I cannot say anything very favourable. The powers of Congreve seem to desert him when he leaves the stage, as Antaeus was no longer strong than when he could touch the ground. It cannot be observed without wonder, that a mind so vigorous and fertile in dramatic compositions should on any other occasion discover nothing but impotence and poverty. He has in these little pieces neither elevation of fancy, selection of language, nor skill in versification: yet, if I were required to select from the whole mass of English poetry the most poetical paragraph, I know not what I could prefer to an exclamation in the "Mourning Bride":-

ALMERIA.

It was a fancied noise; for all is hushed.

LEONORA.

It bore the accent of a human voice.

ALMERIA.

It was thy fear, or else some transient wind Whistling through hollows of this vaulted isle: We'll listen -

LEONORA.

Hark!

ALMERIA.

No, all is hushed and still as death.--'Tis dreadful! How reverend is the face of this tall pile, Whose ancient pillars rear their marble heads, To bear aloft its arched and ponderous roof, By its own weight made steadfast and immovable, Looking tranquillity! It strikes an awe And terror on my aching sight; the tombs And monumental caves of death look cold, And shoot a chillness to my trembling heart. Give use thy hand, and let me hear thy voice; Nay, quickly speak to me, and let me hear Thy voice--my own affrights me with its echoes.

He who reads these lines enjoys for a moment the powers of a poet; he feels what he remembers to have felt before, but he feels it with great increase of sensibility; he recognises a familiar image, but meets it again amplified and expanded, embellished with beauty and enlarged with majesty. Yet could the author, who appears here to have enjoyed the confidence of Nature, lament the death of Queen Mary in lines like these:-

"The rocks are cleft, and new-descending rills Furrow the brows of all the impending hills. The water-gods to floods their rivulets turn, And each, with streaming eyes, supplies his wanting urn. The fauns forsake the woods, the nymphs the grove, And round the plain in sad distractions rove: In prickly brakes their tender limbs they tear, And leave on thorns their locks of golden hair. With their sharp nails, themselves the satyrs wound, And tug their shaggy beards, and bite with grief the ground. Lo Pan himself, beneath a blasted oak, Dejected lies, his pipe in pieces broke See Pales weeping too in wild despair, And to the piercing winds her bosses bare. And see yon fading myrtle, where appears The Queen of Love, all bathed in flowing tears; See how she wrings her hands, and beats her breast, And tears her useless girdle from her waist: Hear the sad murmurs of her sighing doves! For grief they sigh, forgetful of their loves."

And many years after he gave no proof that time had improved his wisdom or his wit, for, on the death of the Marquis of Blandford, this was his song:-

"And now the winds, which had so long been still, Began the swelling air with sighs to fill; The water-nymphs, who motionless remained Like images of ice, while she complained, Now loosed their streams; as when descending rains Roll the steep torrents headlong o'er the plains. The prone creation who so long had gazed Charmed with her cries, and at her griefs amazed, Began to roar and howl with horrid yell, Dismal to hear, and terrible to tell! Nothing but groans and sighs were heard around, And echo multiplied each mournful sound."

In both these funeral poems, when he has YELLED out many SYLLABLES of senseless DOLOUR, he dismisses his reader with senseless consolation. From the grave of Pastora rises a light that forms a star, and where Amaryllis wept for Amyntas from every tear sprung up a violet. But William is his hero, and of William he will sing:-

"The hovering winds on downy wings shall wait around, And catch, and waft to foreign lands, the flying sound."

It cannot but be proper to show what they shall have to catch and carry:-

"'Twas now, when flowery lawns the prospect made, And flowing brooks beneath a forest shade, A lowing heifer, loveliest of the herd, Stood feeding by; while two fierce bulls prepared Their armed heads for light, by fate of war to prove The victor worthy of the fair one's love; Unthought presage of what met next my view; For soon the shady scene withdrew. And now, for woods, and fields, and springing flowers, Behold a town arise, bulwarked with walls and lofty towers; Two rival armies all the plain o'erspread, Each in battalia ranged, and shining arms arrayed With eagle eyes beholding both from far, Namur, the price and mistress of the war."

The "Birth of the Muse" is a miserable fiction. One good line it has which was borrowed from Dryden. The concluding verses are these:-

"This said, no more remained. The ethereal host Again impatient crowd the crystal coast. The father now, within his spacious hands, Encompassed all the mingled mass of seas and lands; And, having heaved aloft the ponderous sphere, He launched the world to float in ambient air."

Of his irregular poems, that to Mrs. Arabella Hunt seems to be the best; his Ode for St. Cecilia's Day, however, had some lines which Pope had in his mind when he wrote his own. His imitations of Horace are feebly paraphrastical, and the additions which he makes are of little value. He sometimes retains what were more properly omitted, as when he talks of VERVAIN and GUMS to propitiate Venus.

Of his Translations, the "Satire of Juvenal" was written very early, and may therefore be forgiven, though it had not the massiness and vigour of the original. In all his versions strength and sprightliness are wanting; his "Hymn to Venus," from Homer, is perhaps the best. His lines are weakened with expletives, and his rhymes are frequently imperfect. His petty poems are seldom worth the cost of criticism; sometimes the thoughts are false and sometimes common. In his verses on Lady Gethin, the latter part is in imitation of Dryden's ode on Mrs. Killigrew; and "Doris," that has been so lavishly flattered by Steele, has indeed some lively stanzas, but the expression might be mended, and the most striking part of the character had been already shown in "Love for Love." His "Art of Pleasing" is founded on a vulgar, but perhaps impracticable principle, and the staleness of the sense is not concealed by any novelty of illustration or elegance of diction. This tissue of poetry, from which he seems to have hoped a lasting name, is totally neglected, and known only as it is appended to his plays.

While comedy or while tragedy is regarded, his plays are likely to be read; but, except what relates to the stage, I know not that he has ever written a stanza that is sung, or a couplet that is quoted. The general character of his "Miscellanies" is that they show little wit and little virtue. Yet to him it must be confessed that we are indebted for the connection of a national error, and for the cure of our Pindaric madness. He first taught the English writers that Pindar's odes were regular; and though certainly he had not the lire requisite for the higher species of lyric poetry, he has shown us that enthusiasm has its rules, and that in mere confusion there is neither grace nor greatness.

BLACKMORE

Sir Richard Blackmore is one of those men whose writings have attracted much notice, but of whose life and manners very little has been communicated, and whose lot it has been to be much oftener mentioned by enemies than by friends. He was the son of Robert Blackmore, of Corsham in Wiltshire, styled by Wood Gentleman, and supposed to have been an attorney, having been for some time educated in a country school, he was at thirteen sent to Westminster, and in 1668 was entered at Edmund Hall in Oxford, where he took the degree of MA. June 8, 1676, and resided thirteen years, a much longer time than is usual to spend at the university, and which he seems to have passed with very little attention to the business of the place; for, in his poems, the ancient names of nations or places, which he often introduces, are pronounced by chance. He afterwards travelled. At Padua he was made doctor of physic, and, after having wandered about a year and a half on the Continent, returned home.

In some part of his life, it is not known when, his indigence compelled him to teach a school, a humiliation with which, though it certainly lasted but a little while, his enemies did not forget to reproach him, when he became conspicuous enough to excite malevolence; and let it be remembered for his honour, that to have been once a schoolmaster is the only reproach which all the perspicacity of malice, animated by wit, has ever fixed upon his private life.

When he first engaged in the study of physic, he inquired, as he says, of Dr. Sydenham, what authors he should read and was directed by Sydenham to "Don Quixote": "which" said he, "is a very good book; I read it still." The perverseness of mankind makes it often mischievous to men of eminence to give way to merriment; the idle and the illiterate will long shelter themselves under this foolish apophthegm. Whether he rested satisfied with this direction, or sought for better, he commenced physician, and obtained high eminence and extensive practice. He became Fellow of the College of Physicians, April 12, 1687, being one of the thirty which, by the new charter of King James, were added to the former fellows. His residence was in Cheapside, and his friends were chiefly in the City. In the early part of Blackmore's time a citizen was a term of reproach; and his place of abode was another topic, to which his adversaries had recourse in the penury of scandal.

Blackmore, therefore, was made a poet not by necessity but inclination, and wrote not for a livelihood but for fame; or, if he may tell his own motives, for a nobler purpose, to engage poetry in the cause of virtue.

I believe it is peculiar to him that his first public work was an heroic poem. He was not known as a maker of verses till he published (in 1695) "Prince Arthur," in ten books, written, as he relates, "by such catches and starts, and in such occasional uncertain hours as his profession afforded, and for the greatest part in coffee-houses, or in passing up and down the streets." For the latter part of this apology he was accused of writing "to the rumbling of his chariot wheels." He had read, he says, "but little poetry throughout his whole life; and for fifteen years before had not written a hundred verses except one copy of Latin verses in praise of a friend's book." He thinks, and with some reason, that from such a performance perfection cannot be expected; but he finds another reason for the severity of his censurers, which he expresses in language such as Cheapside easily furnished. "I am not free of the Poet's Company, having never kissed the governor's hands: mine is therefore not so much as a permission poem, but a downright interloper. Those gentlemen, who carry on their poetical trade in a joint stock, would certainly do what they could to sink and ruin an unlicensed adventurer, notwithstanding I disturbed none of their factories, nor imported any goods they have ever dealt in." He had lived in the City till he had learned its note.

That "Prince Arthur" found many readers is certain; for in two years it had three editions, a very uncommon instance of favourable reception, at a time when literary curiosity was yet confined to particular classes of the nation. Such success naturally raised animosity; and Dennis attacked it by a formal criticism, more tedious and disgusting than the work which he condemns. To this censure may be opposed the approbation of Locke, and the admiration of Molyneux, which are found in their printed "Letters." Molyneux is particularly delighted with the song of Mopas, which is therefore subjoined to this narrative.

It is remarked by Pope, that "what raises the hero, often sinks the man." Of Blackmore is may be said that, as the poet sinks, the man rises; the animadversions of Dennis, insolent and contemptuous as they were, raised in him no implacable resentment; he and his critic were afterwards friends; and in one of his latter works he praises Dennis "as equal to Boileau in poetry, and superior to him in critical abilities." He seems to have been more delighted with praise than pained by censure, and instead of slackening, quickened his career. Having in two years produced ten books of "Prince Arthur," in two years more (1697) he sent into the world "King Arthur" in twelve. The provocation was now doubled, and the resentment of wits and critics may be supposed to have increased in proportion. He found, however, advantages more than equivalent to all their outrages. He was this year made one of the physicians in ordinary to King William, and advanced by him to the honour of knighthood, with the present of a gold chaise and medal. The malignity of the wits attributed his knighthood to his new poem, but King William was not very studious of poetry; and Blackmore perhaps had other merit, for he says in his dedication to "Alfred," that "he had a greater part in the succession of the house of Hanover than ever he had boasted."

What Blackmore could contribute to the Succession, or what he imagined himself to have contributed, cannot now be known. That he had been of considerable use, I doubt not but he believed, for I hold him to have been very honest; but he might easily make a false estimate of his own importance. Those whom their virtue restrains from deceiving others, are often disposed by their vanity to deceive themselves. Whether he promoted the Succession or not, he at least approved it, and adhered invariably to his principles and party through his whole life.

His ardour of poetry still continued; and not long after (1700) he published a "Paraphrase on the Book of Job, and other parts of the Scripture." This performance Dryden, who pursued him with great malignity, lived long enough to ridicule in a Prologue.

The wits easily confederated against him, as Dryden, whose favour they almost all courted, was his professed adversary. He had, besides, given them reason for resentment, as, in his preface to "Prince Arthur," he had said of the dramatic writers almost all that was alleged afterwards by Collier; but Blackmore's censure was cold and general, Collier's was personal and ardent; Blackmore taught his reader to dislike what Collier incited him to abhor.

In his preface to "King Arthur" he endeavoured to gain at least one friend, and propitiated Congreve by higher praise of his "Mourning Bride" than it has obtained from any other critic.

The same year he published a "Satire on Wit," a proclamation of defiance which united the poets almost all against him, and which brought upon him lampoons and ridicule from every side. This he doubtless foresaw, and evidently despised; nor should his dignity of mind be without its praise, had he not paid the homage to greatness which he denied to genius, and degraded himself by conferring that authority over the national taste, which he takes from the poets, upon men of high rank and wide influence, but of less wit and not greater virtue.

Here is again discovered the inhabitant of Cheapside, whose head cannot keep his poetry unmingled with trade. To hinder that intellectual bankruptcy which he affects to fear he will erect a "Bank for Wit." In this poem he justly censured Dryden's impurities, but praised his powers, though in a subsequent edition he retained the satire, and omitted the praise. What was his reason, I know not; Dryden was then no longer in his way. His head still teemed with heroic poetry; and (1705) he published "Eliza," in ten books. I am afraid that the world was now weary of contending about Blackmore's heroes, for I do not remember that by any author, serious or comical, I have found "Eliza" either praised or blamed.

She "dropped," as it seems, "dead-born from the press." It is never mentioned, and was never seen by me till I borrowed it for the present occasion. Jacob says "it is corrected and revised from another impression," but the labour of revision was thrown away.

From this time he turned some of his thoughts to the celebration of living characters, and wrote a poem on the Kit-Cat Club, and "Advice to the Poets how to celebrate the Duke of Marlborough" but on occasion of another year of success, thinking himself qualified to give more instruction, he again wrote a poem of "Advice to a Weaver of Tapestry." Steele was then publishing the Tatler, and, looking round him for something at which he might laugh, unluckily alighted on Sir Richard's work, and treated it with such contempt that, as Fenton observes, he put an end to that species of writers that gave advice to painters.

Not long after (1712) he published "Creation," a philosophical poem, which has been, by my recommendation, inserted in the late collection. Whoever judges of this by any other of Blackmore's performances will do it injury. The praise given it by Addison (Spectator, 339) is too well known to be transcribed; but some notice is due to the testimony of Dennis, who calls it a "philosophical poem, which has equalled that of 'Lucretius' in the beauty of its versification, and infinitely surpassed it in the solidity and strength of its reasoning."

Why an author surpasses himself it is natural to inquire. I have heard from Mr. Draper, an eminent bookseller, an account received by him from Ambrose Philips, "That Blackmore, as he proceeded in this poem, laid his manuscript from time to time before a club of wits with whom he associated, and that every man contributed, as he could, either improvement or correction; so that," said Philips, "there are perhaps nowhere in the book thirty lines together that now stand as they were originally written."

The relation of Philips, I suppose, was true; but when all reasonable, all credible allowance is made for this friendly revision, the author will still retain an ample dividend of praise; for to him must always be assigned the plan of the work, the distribution of its parts, the choice of topics, the train of argument, and, what is yet more, the general predominance of philosophical judgment and poetical spirit. Correction seldom effects more than the suppression of faults: a happy line, or a single elegance, may perhaps be added; but of a large work, the general character must always remain. The original constitution can be very little helped by local remedies; inherent and radical dulness will never be much invigorated by intrinsic animation. This poem, if he had written nothing else, would have transmitted him to posterity among the first favourites of the English muse; but to make verses was his transcendent pleasure, and, as he was not deterred by censure, he was not satiated with praise. He deviated, however, sometimes into other tracks of literature, and condescended to entertain his readers with plain prose. When the Spectator stopped, he considered the polite world as destitute of entertainment, and in concert with Mr. Hughes, who wrote every third paper, published three times a week the "Lay Monastery," founded on the supposition that some literary men, whose characters are described, had retired to a house in the country to enjoy philosophical leisure, and resolved to instruct the public by communicating their disquisitions and amusements. Whether any real persons were concealed under fictitious names is not known. The hero of the club is one Mr. Johnson, such a constellation of excellence, that his character shall not be suppressed, though there is no great genius in the design nor skill in the delineation.

"The first I shall name is Mr. Johnson, a gentleman that owes to nature excellent faculties and an elevated genius, and to industry and application many acquired accomplishments. His taste is distinguishing, just, and delicate; his judgment clear, and his reason strong, accompanied with an imagination full of spirit, of great compass, and stored with refined ideas. He is a critic of the first rank and, what is his peculiar ornament, he is delivered from the ostentation, malevolence, and supercilious temper, that so often blemish men of that character. His remarks result from the nature and reason of things, and are formed by a judgment free and unbiassed by the authority of those who have lazily followed each other in the same beaten track of thinking, and are arrived only at the reputation of acute grammarians and commentators; men who have been copying one another many hundred years without any improvement, or, if they have ventured farther, have only applied in a mechanical manner the rules of ancient critics to modern writings, and with great labour discovered nothing but their own want of judgment and capacity. As Mr. Johnson penetrates to the bottom of his subject, by which means his observations are solid and natural, as well as delicate, so his design is always to bring to light something useful and ornamental; whence his character is the reverse to theirs, who have eminent abilities in insignificant knowledge, and a great felicity in finding out trifles. He is no less industrious to search out the merit of an author, than sagacious in discerning his errors and defects, and takes more pleasure in commending the beauties than exposing the blemishes of a laudable writing. Like Horace, in a long work he can bear some deformities, and justly lay them on the imperfection of human nature, which is incapable of faultless productions. When an excellent drama appears in public, and by its intrinsic worth attracts a general applause, he is not stung with envy and spleen; nor does he express a savage nature in fastening upon the celebrated author, dwelling upon his imaginary defects, and passing over his conspicuous excellences. He treats all writers upon the same impartial foot, and is not, like the little critics, taken up entirely in finding out only the beauties of the ancient and nothing but the errors of the modern writers. Never did any one express more kindness and good-nature to young and unfinished authors, he promotes their interests, protects their reputation, extenuates their faults, and sets off their virtues, and by his candour guards them from the severity of his judgment. He is not like those dry critics who are morose because they cannot write themselves, but is himself master of a good vein in poetry; and though he does not often employ it, yet he has sometimes entertained his friends with his unpublished performances."

The rest of the lay monks seem to be but feeble mortals an comparison with the gigantic Johnson, who yet, with all his abilities and the help of the fraternity, could drive the publication but to forty papers, which were afterwards collected into a volume, and called in the title "A Sequel to the Spectators."

Some years afterwards (1716 and 1717) he published two volumes of essays in prose, which can be commended only as they are written for the highest and noblest purpose--the promotion of religion. Blackmore's prose is not the prose of a poet, for it is languid, sluggish, and lifeless; his diction is neither daring nor exact, his flow neither rapid nor easy, and his periods neither smooth nest strong. His account of WIT will show with how little clearness he is content to think, and how little his thoughts are recommended by his language.

"As to its efficient cause, WIT owes its production to an extraordinary and peculiar temperament in the constitution of the possessor of it, in which is found a concurrence of regular and exalted ferments, and an affluence of animal spirits, refined and rectified to a great degree of purity; whence, being endowed with vivacity, brightness, and celerity, as well in their reflections as direct motions, they become proper instruments for the sprightly operations of the mind, by which means the imagination can with great facility range the wide field of Nature, contemplate an infinite variety of objects, and, by observing the similitude and disagreement of their several qualities, single out and abstract, and then suit and unite, those ideas which will best serve its purpose. Hence beautiful allusions, surprising metaphors, and admirable sentiments, are always ready at hand; and while the fancy is full of images, collected from innumerable objects, and their different qualities, relations, and habitudes, it can at pleasure dress a common notion in a strange but becoming garb, by which, as before observed, the same thought will appear a new one, to the great delight and wonder of the hearer. What we call genius results from this particular happy complexion in the first formation of the person that enjoys it, and is Nature's gift, but diversified by various specific characters and limitations, as its active fire is blended and allayed by different proportions of phlegm, or reduced and regulated by the contrast of opposite ferments. Therefore, as there happens in the composition of facetious genius a greater or less, though still an inferior, degree of judgment and prudence, one man of wit will be varied and distinguished from another."

In these essays he took little care to propitiate the wits, for he scorns to avert their malice at the expense of virtue or of truth.

"Several, in their books, have many sarcastical and spiteful strokes at religion in general; while others make themselves pleasant with the principles of the Christian. Of the last kind this age has seen a most audacious example in the book entitled 'A Tale of a Tub.' Had this writing been published in a pagan or popish nation, who are justly impatient of all indignity offered to the established religion of their country, no doubt but the author would have received the punishment he deserved. But the fate of this impious buffoon is very different, for in a Protestant kingdom, zealous of their civil and religious immunities, he has not only escaped affronts and the effects of public resentment, but has been caressed and patronised by persons of great figure, and of all denominations. Violent party-men, who differed in all things besides, agreed in their turn to show particular respect and friendship to this insolent derider of the worship of his country, till at last the reputed writer is not only gone off with impunity, but triumphs in his dignity and preferment. I do not know that any inquiry or search was ever made after this writing, or that any reward was ever offered for the discovery of the author, or that the infamous book was ever condemned to be burnt in public. Whether this proceeds from the excessive esteem and love that men in power, during the late reign, had for wit, or their defect of zeal and concern for the Christian religion will be determined best by those who are best acquainted with their character."

In another place he speaks with becoming abhorrence of a GODLESS AUTHOR who has burlesqued a Psalm. This author was supposed to be Pope, who published a reward for any one that would produce the coiner of the accusation, but never denied it, and was afterwards the perpetual and incessant enemy of Blackmore.

One of his essays is upon the spleen, which is treated by him so much to his own satisfaction, that he has published the same thoughts in the same words; first, in the "Lay Monastery," then in the "Essay," and then in the "Preface to a Medical Treatise on the Spleen." One passage, which I have found already twice, I will here exhibit, because I think it better imagined and better expressed than could be expected from the common tenor of his prose:-

"--As the several combinations of splenetic madness and folly produce an infinite variety of irregular under-standing, so the amicable accommodation and alliance between several virtues and vices produce an equal diversity in the dispositions and manners of mankind; whence it comes to pass, that as many monstrous and absurd productions are found in the moral as in the intellectual world. How surprising is it to observe among the least culpable men, some whose minds are attracted by heaven and earth with a seeming equal force; some who are proud of humility; others who are censorious and uncharitable, yet self-denying and devout; some who join contempt of the world with sordid avarice; and others, who preserve a great degree of piety with ill-nature and ungoverned passions. Nor are instances of this inconsistent mixture less frequent among bad men, where we often with admiration see persons at once generous and unjust, impious lovers of their country, and flagitious heroes, good-natured sharpers, immoral men of honour, and libertines who will sooner die than change their religion; and though it is true that repugnant coalitions of so high a degree are found but in a part of mankind, yet none of the whole mass, either good or bad, are entirely exempted from some absurd mixture."

He about this time (August 22, 1716) became one of the elects of the College of Physicians, and was soon after (October 1) chosen Censor. He seems to have arrived late, whatever was the reason, at his medical honours.

Having succeeded so well in his book on Creation, by which he established the great principle of all religion, he thought his undertaking imperfect, unless he likewise enforced the truth of Revelation, and for that purpose added another poem on "Redemption." He had likewise written before his "Creation" three books on the Nature of Man.

The lovers of musical devotion have always wished for a more happy metrical version than they have yet obtained of the Book of Psalms. This wish the piety of Blackmore led him to gratify, and he produced (1721) "A New Version of the Psalms of David fitted to the Tunes used in Churches," which being recommended by the archbishops and many bishops, obtained a license for its admission into public worship; but no admission has it yet obtained, nor has it any right to come where Brady and Tate have got possession. Blackmore's name must be added to those of many others who, by the same attempt, have obtained only the praise of meaning well.

He was not yet deterred from heroic poetry. There was another monarch of this island (for he did not fetch his heroes from foreign countries) whom he considered as worthy the epic muse, and he dignified "Alfred" (1723) with twelve books. But the opinion of the nation was now settled; a hero introduced by Blackmore was not likely to find either respect or kindness; "Alfred" took his place by "Eliza" in silence and darkness. Benevolence was ashamed to favour, and malice was weary of insulting. Of his four epic poems, the first had such reputation and popularity as enraged the critics; the second was at least known enough to be ridiculed; the two last had neither friends nor enemies.

Contempt is a kind of gangrene, which, if it seizes one part of a character, corrupts all the rest by degrees. Blackmore being despised as a poet, was in time neglected as a physician; his practice, which was once invidiously great, forsook him in the latter part of his life, but being by nature, or by principle, averse from idleness, he employed his unwelcome leisure in writing books on physic, and teaching others to cure those whom he could himself cure no longer. I know not whether I can enumerate all the treatises by which he has endeavoured to diffuse the art of healing, for there is scarcely any distemper of dreadful name which he has not taught the reader how to oppose. He has written on the small-pox, with a vehement invective against inoculation; on consumption, the spleen, the gout, the rheumatism, the king's evil, the dropsy, the jaundice, the stone, the diabetes, and the plague. Of those books, if I had read them, it could nor be expected that I should be able to give a critical account. I have been told that there is something in them of vexation and discontent, discovered by a perpetual attempt to degrade physic from its sublimity, and to represent it as attainable without much previous or concomitant learning. By the transient glances which I have thrown upon them I have observed an affected contempt of the ancients, and a supercilious derision of transmitted knowledge. Of this indecent arrogance the following quotation from his preface to the "Treatise on the Small-pox" will afford a specimen, in which, when the reader finds what I fear is true, that, when he was censuring Hippocrates, he did not know the difference between aphorism and apophthegm, he will not pay much regard to his determinations concerning ancient learning.

"As for this book of aphorisms, it is like my Lord Bacon's of the same title, a book of jests, or a grave collection of trite and trifling observations; of which, though many are true and certain, yet they signify nothing, and may afford diversion, but no instruction, most of them being much inferior to the sayings of the wise men of Greece, which yet are so low and mean, that we are entertained every day with more valuable sentiments at the table conversation of ingenious and learned men."

I am unwilling, however, to leave him in total disgrace, and will therefore quote from another preface a passage less reprehensible.

"Some gentlemen have been disingenuous and unjust to me, by wresting and forcing my meaning, in the preface to another book, as if I condemned and exposed all learning, though they knew I declared that I greatly honoured and esteemed all men of superior literature and erudition, and that I only undervalued false or superficial learning, that signifies nothing for the service of mankind; and that as to physic, I expressly affirmed that learning must be joined with native genius to make a physician of the first rank; but if those talents are separated, I asserted, and do still insist, that a man of native sagacity and diligence will prove a more able and useful practiser than a heavy notional scholar, encumbered with a heap of confused ideas."

He was not only a poet and a physician, but produced likewise a work of a different kind, "A True and Impartial History of the Conspiracy against King William of Glorious Memory in the Year 1695." This I have never seen, but suppose it is at least compiled with integrity. He engaged likewise in theological controversy, and wrote two books against the Arians: "Just Prejudices against the Arian Hypothesis," and "Modern Arians Unmasked." Another of his works is "Natural Theology; or, Moral Duties considered apart from Positive; with some Observations on the Desirableness and Necessity of a Supernatural Revelation." This was the last book that he published. He left behind him "The Accomplished Preacher; or, an Essay upon Divine Eloquence," which was printed after his death by Mr. White of Nayland, in Essex, the minister who attended his death-bed, and testified the fervent piety of his last hours. He died on the 8th of October, 1729.

Blackmore, by the unremitted enmity of the wits, whom he provoked more by his virtue than his dulness, has been exposed to worse treatment than he deserved. His name was so long used to point every epigram upon dull writers, that it became at last a byword of contempt but it deserves observation, that malignity takes hold only of his writings, and that his life passed without reproach, even when his boldness of reprehension naturally turned upon him many eyes desirous to espy faults which many tongues would have made haste to publish. But those who could not blame, could, at least, forbear to praise, and therefore of his private life and domestic character there are no memorials.

As an author, he may justly claim the honours of magnanimity. The incessant attacks of his enemies, whether serious or merry, are never discovered to have disturbed his quiet, or to have lessened his confidence in himself: they neither awed him to silence nor to caution: they neither provoked him to petulance, nor depressed him to complaint. While the distributors of literary fame were endeavouring to depreciate and degrade him, he either despised or defied them, wrote on as he had written before, and never turned aside to quiet them by civility, or repress them by confutation. He depended with great security on his own powers, and perhaps was for that reason less diligent in perusing books. His literature was, I think, but small. What he knew of antiquity, I suspect him to have gathered from modern compilers; but, though he could not boast of much critical knowledge, his mind was stored with general principles, and he left minute researches to those whom he considered as little minds. With this disposition he wrote most of his poems. Having formed a magnificent design, he was careless of particular and subordinate elegances; he studied no niceties of versification; he waited for no felicities of fancy, but caught his first thoughts in the first words in which they were presented; nor does it appear that he saw beyond his own performances, or had ever elevated his was to that ideal perfection which every genius born to excel is condemned always to pursue, and never overtake. In the first suggestions of his imagination he acquiesced; he thought them good, and did not seek for better. His works may be read a long time without the occurrence of a single line that stands prominent from the rest. The poem on "Creation" has, however, the appearance of more circumspection; it wants neither harmony of numbers, accuracy of thought, nor elegance of diction. It has either been written with great care, or, what cannot be imagined of so long a work, with such felicity as made care less necessary. Its two constituent parts are ratiocination and description. To reason in verse is allowed to be difficult; but Blackmore not only reasons in verse, but very often reasons poetically; and finds the art of uniting ornament with strength and ease with closeness. This is a skill which Pope might have condescended to learn from him, when he needed it so much in his "Moral Essays."

In his descriptions both of life and nature, the poet and the philosopher happily co-operate; truth is recommended by elegance, and elegance sustained by truth. In the structure and order of the poem, not only the greater parts are properly consecutive, but the didactic and illustrative paragraphs are so happily mingled, that labour is relieved by pleasure, and the attention is led on through a long succession of varied excellence to the original position, the fundamental principle of wisdom and of virtue.

As the heroic poems of Blackmore are now little read, it is thought proper to insert, as a specimen from "Prince Arthur," the song of Mopas mentioned by Molyneux:-

"But that which Arthur with most pleasure heard Were noble strains, by Mopas sung the bard, Who to his harp in lofty verse began, And through the secret maze of Nature ran. He the Great Spirit sung, that all things filled, That the tumultuous waves of Chaos stilled; Whose nod disposed the jarring seeds to peace, And made the wars of hostile Atoms cease. All Beings, we in fruitful Nature find, Proceeded from the Great Eternal mind: Streams of his unexhausted spring of power, And, cherished with his influence, endure. He spread the pure cerulean fields on high, And arched the chambers of the vaulted sky, Which he, to suit their glory with their height, Adorned with globes, that reel, as drunk with light. His hand directed all the tuneful spheres, He turned their orbs, and polished all the stars. He filled the Sun's vast lamp with golden light: And bid the silver Moon adorn the night. He spread the airy Ocean without shores, Where birds are wafted with their feathered oars. Then sung the bard how the light vapours rise From the warm earth, and cloud the smiling skies; He sung how some, chilled in their airy flight, Fall scattered down in pearly dew by night; How some, raised higher, sit in secret steams On the reflected points of bounding beams, Till, chilled with cold, they shade th' ethereal plain, Then on the thirsty earth descend in rain; How some, whose parts a slight contexture show, Sink hovering through the air in fleecy snow; How part is spun in silken threads, and clings Entangled in the grass is gluey strings; How others stamp to stones, with rushing sound Fall from their crystal quarries to the ground; How some are laid in trains, that kindled fly, In harmless fires by night, about the sky; How some in winds blow with impetuous force, And carry ruin where they bend their course, While some conspire to form a gentle breeze, To fan the air, and play among the trees; How some, enraged, grow turbulent and loud, Pent in the bowels of a frowning cloud, That cracks, as if the axis of the world Was broke, and Heaven's bright towers were downwards hurled. He sung how earth's wide ball, at Jove's command, Did in the midst on airy columns stand; And how the soul of plants, in prison held, And bound with sluggish fetters, lies concealed, Till with the spring's warm beams, almost released From the dull weight, with which it lay opprest, Its vigour spreads, and makes the teeming earth Heave up, and labour with the sprouting birth: The active spirit freedom seeks in vain, It only works and twists a stronger chain; Urging its prison's sides to break a way, It makes that wider, where 'tis forced to stay: Till, having formed its living house, it rears Its head, and in a tender plant appears. Hence springs the oak, the beauty of the grove, Whose stately trunk fierce storms can scarcely move. Hence grows the cedar, hence the swelling vine Does round the elm its purple clusters twine. Hence painted flowers the smiling gardens bless, Both with their fragrant scent and gaudy dress. Hence the white lily in full beauty grows, Hence the blue violet and blushing rose. He sung how sunbeams brood upon the earth, And in the glebe hatch such a numerous birth; Which way the genial warmth in Summer storms Turns putrid vapours to a bed of worms; How rain, transformed by this prolific power, Falls from the clouds an animated shower. He sung the embryo's growth within the womb, And how the parts their various shapes assume. With what rare art the wondrous structure's wrought, From one crude mass to such perfection brought; That no part useless, none misplaced we see, None are forgot, and more would monstrous be."

POPE

Alexander Pope was born in London, May 22, 1688, of parents whose rank or station was never ascertained: we are informed that they were of "gentle blood;" that his father was of a family of which the Earl of Downe was the head, and that his mother was the daughter of William Turner, Esquire, of York, who had likewise three sons, one of whom had the honour of being killed, and the other of dying, in the service of Charles the First; the third was made a general officer in Spain, from whom the sister inherited what sequestrations and forfeitures had left in the family. This, and this only, is told by Pope, who is more willing, as I have heard observed, to show what his father was not, than what he was. It is allowed that he grew rich by trade; but whether in a shop or on the Exchange was never discovered till Mr. Tyers told, on the authority of Mrs. Racket, that he was a linendraper in the Strand. Both parents were Papists.

Pope was from his birth of a constitution tender and delicate, but is said to have shown remarkable gentleness and sweetness of disposition. The weakness of his body continued through his life, but the mildness of his mind perhaps ended with his childhood. His voice when he was young was so pleasing, that he was called in fondness "The Little Nightingale."

Being not sent early to school, he was taught to read by an aunt; and, when he was seven or eight years old, became a lover of books. He first learned to write by imitating printed books, a species of penmanship in which he retained great excellence through his whole life, though his ordinary hand was not elegant. When he was about eight he was placed in Hampshire, under Taverner, a Romish priest, who, by a method very rarely practised, taught him the Greek and Latin rudiments together. He was now first regularly initiated in poetry by the perusal of "Ogilby's Homer" and "Sandys' Ovid." Ogilby's assistance he never repaid with any praise; but of Sandys he declared, in his notes to the "Iliad," that English poetry owed much of its beauty to his translations. Sandys very rarely attempted original composition.

From the care of Taverner, under whom his proficiency was considerable, he was removed to a school at Twyford, near Winchester, and again to another school about Hyde Park Corner, from which he used sometimes to stroll to the play-hones, and was so delighted with theatrical exhibitions, that he formed a kind of play from "Ogilby's Iliad," with some verses of his own intermixed, which he persuaded his schoolfellows to act, with the addition of his master's gardener, who personated Ajax.

At the two last schools he used to represent himself as having lost part of what Taverner had taught him, and on his master at Twyford he had already exercised his poetry in a lampoon. Yet under those masters he translated more than a fourth part of the "Metamorphoses." If he kept the same proportion in his other exercises, it cannot be thought that his loss was great. He tells of himself, in his poems, that "he lisped in numbers;" and used to say that he could not remember the time when he began to make verses. In the style of fiction, it might have been said of him, as of Pindar, that when he lay in his cradle "the bees swarmed about his mouth."

About the time of the Revolution his father, who was undoubtedly disappointed by the sudden blast of Popish prosperity, quitted his trade, and retired to Binfield, in Windsor Forest, with about twenty thousand pounds, for which, being conscientiously determined not to entrust it to the Government, he found no better use than that of locking it up in a chest, and taking from it what his expenses required; and his life was long enough to consume a great part of it before his son came to the inheritance.

To Binfield Pope was called by his father when he was about twelve years old, and there he had for a few months the assistance of one Deane, another priest, of whom he learned only to construe a little of "Tully's Offices." How Mr. Deane could spend with a boy who had translated so much of "Ovid" some months over a small part of "Tully's Offices," it is now vain to inquire. Of a youth so successfully employed, and so conspicuously improved, a minute account must be naturally desired; but curiosity must be contented with confused, imperfect, and sometimes improbable intelligence. Pope, finding little advantage from external help, resolved thenceforward to direct himself, and at twelve formed a plan of study, which he completed with little other incitement than the desire of excellence. His primary and principal purpose was to be a poet, with which his father accidentally concurred by proposing subjects and obliging him to correct his performances by many revisals, after which the old gentleman, when he was satisfied, would say, "These are good rhymes." In his perusal of the English poets he soon distinguished the versification of Dryden, which he considered as the model to be studied, and was impressed with such veneration for his instructor, that he persuaded some friends to take him to the coffee-house which Dryden frequented, and pleased himself with having seen him.

Dryden died May 1, 1701, some days before Pope was twelve; so early must he therefore have felt the power of harmony, and the zeal of genius. Who does not wish that Dryden could have known the value of the homage that was paid him, and foreseen the greatness of his young admirer?

The earliest of Pope's productions is his "Ode on Solitude," written before he was twelve, in which there is nothing more than other forward boys have attained, and which is not equal to Cowley's performance at the same age. His time was now wholly spent in reading and writing. As he read the classics he amused himself with translating them, and at fourteen made a version of the first book of the "Thebais," which, with some revision, he afterwards published. He must have been at this time, if he had no help, a considerable proficient in the Latin tongue.

By Dryden's fables, which had then been not long published, and were much in the hands of poetical readers, he was tempted to try his own skill in giving Chaucer a more fashionable appearance, and put "January and May" and the "Prologue of the Wife of Bath" into modern English. He translated likewise the Epistle of "Sappho to Phaon" from Ovid, to complete the version, which was before imperfect, and wrote some other small pieces, which he afterwards printed. He sometimes imitated the English poets, and professed to have written at fourteen his poem upon "Silence," after Rochester's "Nothing." He had now formed his versification, and the smoothness of his numbers surpassed his original; but this is a small part of his praise; he discovers such acquaintance both with human life and public affairs as is not easily conceived to have been attainable by a boy of fourteen in Windsor Forest.

Next year he was desirous of opening to himself new sources of knowledge, by making himself acquainted with modern languages, and removed for a time to London, that he might study French and Italian, which, as he desired nothing more than to read them, were by diligent application soon despatched. Of Italian learning he does not appear to have ever made much use in his subsequent studies. He then returned to Binfield, and delighted himself with his own poetry. He tried all styles, and many subjects. He wrote a comedy, a tragedy, an epic poem, with panegyrics on all the princes of Europe; and, as he confesses, "thought himself the greatest genius that ever was." Self-confidence is the first requisite to great undertakings. He, indeed, who forms his opinion of himself in solitude, without knowing the powers of other men, is very liable to error; but it was the felicity of Pope to rate himself at his real value. Most of his puerile productions were, by his maturer judgment, afterwards destroyed. "Alcander," the epic poem, was burnt by the persuasion of Atterbury. The tragedy was founded on the legend of St. Genevieve. Of the comedy there is no account. Concerning his studies, it is related that he translated "Tully on Old Age," and that, besides his books of poetry and criticisms, he read

"Temple's Essays" and "Locke on Human Understanding." His reading, though his favourite authors are not known, appears to have been sufficiently extensive and multifarious, for his early pieces show with sufficient evidence his knowledge of books. He that is pleased with himself easily imagines that he shall please others. Sir William Trumbull, who had been Ambassador at Constantinople, and Secretary of State, when he retired from business, fixed his residence in the neighbourhood of Binfield. Pope, not yet sixteen, was introduced to the statesman of sixty, and so distinguished himself that their interviews ended in friendship and correspondence. Pope was, through his whole life, ambitious of splendid acquaintance; and he seems to have wanted neither diligence nor success in attracting the notice of the great, for, from his first entrance into the world, and his entrance was very early, he was admitted to familiarity with those whose rank or station made them most conspicuous.

From the age of sixteen the life of Pope, as an author, may be properly computed. He now wrote his pastorals, which were shown to the poets and critics of that time. As they well deserved, they were read with admiration, and many praises were bestowed upon them and upon the preface, which is both elegant and learned in a high degree; they were, however, not published till five years afterwards.

Cowley, Milton, and Pope are distinguished among the English poets by the early exertion of their powers, but the works of Cowley alone were published in his childhood, and, therefore, of him only can it be certain that his puerile performances received no improvement from his maturer studies.

At this time began his acquaintance with Wycherley, a man who seems to have had among his contemporaries his full share of reputation, to have been esteemed without virtue, and caressed without good humour. Pope was proud of his notice. Wycherley wrote verses in his praise, which he was charged by Dennis with writing to himself, and they agreed for a while to flatter one another. It is pleasant to remark how soon Pope learned the cant of an author, and began to treat critics with contempt, though he had yet suffered nothing from them. But the fondness of Wycherley was too violent to last. His esteem of Pope was such that he submitted some poems to his revision, and when Pope, perhaps proud of such confidence, was sufficiently bold in his criticisms, and liberal in his alterations, the old scribbler was angry to see his pages defaced, and felt more pain from the detection than content from the amendment of his faults. They parted, but Pope always considered him with kindness, and visited him a little time before he died. Another of his early correspondents was Mr. Cromwell, of whom I have learned nothing particular, but that he used to ride a-hunting in a tie-wig. He was fond, and perhaps vain, of amusing himself with poetry and criticism, and sometimes sent his performances to Pope, who did not forbear such remarks as were now and then unwelcome. Pope, in his turn, put the juvenile version of "Statius" into his hands for correction. Their correspondence afforded the public its first knowledge of Pope's epistolary powers, for his letters were given by Cromwell to one Mrs. Thomas, and she many years afterwards sold them to Curll, who inserted them in a volume of his "Miscellanies."

Walsh, a name yet preserved among the minor poets, was one of his first encouragers. His regard was gained by the pastorals, and from him Pope received the counsel from which he seems to have regulated his studies. Walsh advised him to correctness, which, as he told him, the English poets had hitherto neglected, and which, therefore, was left to him as a basis of fame; and, being delighted with rural poems, recommended to him to write a pastoral comedy, like those which are read so eagerly in Italy, a design which Pope probably did not approve, as he did not follow it.

Pope had now declared himself a poet, and, thinking himself entitled to poetical conversation, began at seventeen to frequent Will's, a coffee-house on the north side of Russell Street, in Covent Garden, where the wits of that time used to assemble, and where Dryden had, when he lived, been accustomed to preside. During this period of his life he was indefatigably diligent and insatiably curious, wanting health for violent and money for expensive pleasures, and having excited in himself very strong desires of intellectual eminence, he spent much of his time over his books; but he read only to store his mind with facts and images, seizing all that his authors presented with undistinguishing voracity, and with an appetite for knowledge too eager to be nice. In a mind like his, however, all the faculties were at once involuntarily improving. Judgment is forced upon us by experience. He that reads many books must compare one opinion or one style with another; and, when he compares, must necessarily distinguish, reject, and prefer. But the account given by himself of his studies was, that from fourteen to twenty he read only for amusement, from twenty to twenty-seven for improvement and instruction; that in the first part of his time he desired only to know, and in the second he endeavoured to judge.

The Pastorals, which had been for some time handed about among poets and critics, were at last printed (1709) in Tonson's "Miscellany," in a volume which began with the Pastorals of Philips, and ended with those of Pope. The same year was written the "Essay on Criticism," a work which displays such extent of comprehension, such nicety of distinction, such acquaintance with mankind, and such knowledge both of ancient and modern learning, as are not often attained by the maturest age and longest experience. It was published about two years afterwards, and, being praised by Addison in the Spectator, with sufficient liberality, met with so much favour as enraged Dennis, "who," he says, "found himself attacked, without any manner of provocation on his side, and attacked in his person instead of his writings, by one who was wholly a stranger to him, at a time when all the world knew he was persecuted by fortune; and not only saw that this was attempted in a clandestine manner, with the utmost falsehood and calumny, but found that all this was done by a little, affected hypocrite, who had nothing in his mouth at the same time but truth, candour, friendship, good-nature, humanity, and magnanimity. How the attack was clandestine is not easily perceived, nor how his person is depreciated; but he seems to have known something of Pope's character, in whom may be discovered an appetite to talk too frequently of his own virtues. The pamphlet is such as rage might be expected to dictate. He supposes himself to be asked two questions; whether the essay will succeed, and who or what is the author.

Its success he admits to be secured by the false opinions then prevalent; the author he concludes to be "young and raw."

"First, because he discovers a sufficiency beyond his little ability, and hath rashly undertaken a task infinitely above his force. Secondly, while this little author struts and affects the dictatorian air, he plainly shows that at the same time he is under the rod: and, while he pretends to give laws to others, is a pedantic slave to authority and opinion. Thirdly, he hath, like schoolboys, borrowed both from living and dead. Fourthly, he knows not his own mind, and frequently contradicts himself. Fifthly, he is almost perpetually in the wrong."

All these positions he attempts to prove by quotations and remarks; but his desire to do mischief is greater than his power. He has, however, justly criticised some passages in these lines:-

"There are whom Heaven has blessed with store of wit, Yet want as much again to manage it: For wit and judgment ever are at strife--"

It is apparent that wit has two meanings, and that what is wanted, though called wit, is truly judgment. So far Dennis is undoubtedly right: but not content with argument, he will have a little mirth, and triumphs over the first couplet in terms too elegant to be forgotten. "By the way, what rare numbers are here! Would not one swear that this youngster had espoused some antiquated muse, who had sued out a divorce on account of impotence, from some superannuated sinner; and, having been p--d by her former spouse, has got the gout in her decrepit age, which makes her hobble so damnably?" This was the man who would reform a nation sinking into barbarity.

In another place Pope himself allowed that Dennis had detected one of those blunders which are called "bulls." The first edition had this line:-

"What is this wit - Where wanted scorned; and envied where acquired?"

"How," says the critic, "can wit be scorned where it is not? Is not this a figure frequently employed in Hibernian land! The person that wants this wit may indeed be scorned, but the scorn shows the honour which the contemner has for wit." Of this remark Pope made the proper use, by correcting the passage.

I have preserved, I think, all that is reasonable in Dennis's criticism; it remains that justice be done to his delicacy. "For his acquaintance," says Dennis, "he names Mr. Walsh, who had by no means the qualification which this author reckons absolutely necessary to a critic, it being very certain that he was, like this essayer a very indifferent poet; he loved to be well dressed; and I remember a little young gentleman whom Mr. Walsh used to take into his company as a double foil to his person and capacity. Inquire between Sunning Hill and Oakingham, for a young, short, equal, gentleman, the very bow of the God of Love, and tell me whether he be a proper author to make personal reflections? He may extol the ancients, but he has reason to thank the gods that he was born a modern; for had he been born of Grecian parents, and his father consequently had by law had the absolute disposal of him, his life had been no longer than that of one of his poems, the life of half a day. Let the person of a gentleman of his parts be never so contemptible, his inward man is ten times more ridiculous; it being impossible that his outward form, though it be that of downright monkey, should differ so much from human shape as his unthinking, immaterial part does from human understanding." Thus began the hostility between Pope and Dennis, which, though it was suspended for a short time, never was appeased. Pope seems, at first, to have attacked him wantonly; but though he always professed to despise him, he discovers, by mentioning him very often, that he felt his force or his venom.

Of this essay, Pope declared that he did not expect the sale to be quick, because "not one gentleman in sixty, even of liberal education, could understand it." The gentleman, and the education of that time, seem to have been of a lower character than they are of this. He mentioned a thousand copies as a numerous impression.

Dennis was not his only censurer; the zealous Papists thought the monks treated with too much contempt, and Erasmus too studiously praised; but to these objections he had not much regard.

The "Essay," has been translated into French by Hamilton, author of the "Comte de Grammont," whose version was never printed, by Robotham, secretary to the king for Hanover, and by Resnel; and commented by Dr. Warburton, who has discovered in it such order and connection as was not perceived by Addison, nor, as it is said, intended by the author.

Almost every poem, consisting of precepts, is so far arbitrary and immethodical, that many of the paragraphs may change places with no apparent inconvenience; for of two or more positions, depending upon some remote and general principle, there is seldom any cogent reason why one should precede the other. But for the order in which they stand, whatever it be, a little ingenuity may easily give a reason. "It is possible," says Hooker, "that, by long circumduction, from any one truth all truth may be inferred." Of all homogeneous truths, at least of all truths respecting the same general end, in whatever series they may be produced, a concatenation by intermediate ideas may be formed, such as, when it is once shown, shall appear natural; but if this order be reversed, another mode of connection equally spacious may be found or made. Aristotle is praised for naming fortitude first of the cardinal virtues, as that without which no other virtue can steadily be practised; but he might, with equal propriety, have placed prudence and justice before it; since without prudence fortitude is mad; without justice, it is mischievous. As the end of method is perspicuity, that series is sufficiently regular that avoids obscurity; and where there is no obscurity, it will not be difficult to discover method.

In the Spectator was published the "Messiah," which he first submitted to the perusal of Steele, and corrected in compliance with his criticisms. It is reasonable to infer from his "Letters" that the verses on the "Unfortunate Lady" were written about the time when his "Essay" was published. The lady's name and adventures I have sought with fruitless inquiry. I can therefore tell no more than I have learned from Mr. Ruffhead, who writes with the confidence of one who could trust his information. She was a woman of eminent rank and large fortune, the ward of an uncle, who, having given her a proper education, expected, like other guardians, that she should make at least an equal match; and such he proposed to her, but found it rejected in favour of a young gentleman of inferior condition. Having discovered the correspondence between the two lovers, and finding the young lady determined to abide by her own choice, he supposed that separation might do what can rarely be done by arguments, and sent her into a foreign country, where she was obliged to converse only with those from whom her uncle had nothing to fear. Her lover took care to repeat his vows; but his letters were intercepted and carried to her guardian, who directed her to be watched with still greater vigilance, till of this restraint she grow so impatient that she bribed a woman servant to procure her a sword, which she directed to her heart.

From this account, given with evident intention to raise the lady's character, it does not appear that she had any claim to praise nor much to compassion. She seems to have been impatient, violent, and ungovernable. Her uncle's power could not have lasted long; the hour of liberty and choice would have come in time. But her desires were too hot for delay, and she liked self-murder better than suspense. Nor is it discovered that the uncle, whoever he was, is with much justice delivered to posterity as "a false guardian." He seems to have done only that for which a guardian is appointed; he endeavoured to direct his niece till she should be able to direct herself. Poetry has not often been worse employed than in dignifying the amorous fiery of a raving girl.

Not long after he wrote the "Rape of the Lock," the most airy, the most ingenious, and the most delightful off all his compositions, occasioned by a frolic of gallantry, rather too familiar, in which Lord Petre cut off a lock of Mrs. Arabella Fermor's hair. This, whether stealth or violence, was so much resented that the commerce of the two families, before very friendly, was interrupted. Mr. Caryl, a gentleman who, being secretary to King James's queen, had followed his mistress into France, and who, being the author of Sir Solomon Single, a comedy, and some translations, was entitled to the notice of a wit, solicited Pope to endeavour a reconciliation by a ludicrous poem which might bring both the parties to a better temper. In compliance with Caryl's request, though his name was for a long time marked only by the first and last letter, "C--l," a poem of two cantos, was written (1711), as is said, in a fortnight, and sent to the offended lady, who liked it well enough to show it; and, with the usual process of literary transactions, the author, dreading a surreptitious edition, was forced to publish it.

The event is said to have been such as was desired, the pacification and diversion of all to whom it related, except Sir George Brown, who complained with some bitterness that, in the character of Sir Plume, he was made to talk nonsense. Whether all this be true I have some doubt; for at Paris, a few years ago, a niece of Mrs. Fermor, who presided in an English convent, mentioned Pope's work with very little gratitude, rather as an insult than an honour; and she may be supposed to have inherited the opinion of her family. At its first appearance at was termed by Addison "merum sal." Pope, however, saw that it was capable of improvement; and, having luckily contrived to borrow his machinery from the Rosicrucians, imparted the scheme with which his head was teeming to Addison, who told him that his work, as it stood, was "a delicious little thing," and gave him no encouragement to retouch it.

This has been too hastily considered as an instance of Addison's jealousy, for, as he could not guess the conduct of the new design, or the possibilities of pleasure comprised in a fiction of which there had been no examples, he might very reasonably and kindly persuade the author to acquiesce in his own prosperity, and forbear an attempt which he considered as an unnecessary hazard. Addison's counsel was happily rejected. Pope foresaw the future efflorescence of imagery then budding in his mind, and resolved to spare no art or industry of cultivation. The soft luxuriance of his fancy was already shooting, and all the gay varieties of diction were ready at his hand to colour and embellish it. His attempt was justified by its success. The "Rape of the Lock" stands forward, in the classes of literature, as the most exquisite example of ludicrous poetry. Berkeley congratulated him upon the display of powers more truly poetical than he had shown before with elegance of description and justness of precepts he had now exhibited boundless fertility of invention. He always considered the intermixture of the machinery with the action as his most successful exertion of poetical art. He, indeed, could never afterwards produce anything of such unexampled excellence. Those performances, which strike with wonder, are combinations of skilful genius with happy casualty; and it is not likely that any felicity, like the discovery of a new race of preternatural agents, should happen twice to the same man. Of this poem the author was, I think, allowed to enjoy the praise for a long time without disturbance. Many years afterwards Dennis published some remarks upon it with very little force and with no effect; for the opinion of the public was already settled, and it was no longer at the mercy of criticism.

About this time he published the "Temple of Fame," which, as he tells Steele in their correspondence, he had written two years before--that is, when he was only twenty-two years old, an early time of life for so much learning and so much observation as that work exhibits. On this poem Dennis afterwards published some remarks, of which the most reasonable is that some of the lines represent motion as exhibited by sculpture.

Of the Epistle from "Eloisa to Abelard," I do not know the date. His first inclination to attempt a composition of that tender kind arose, as Mr. Savage told me, from his perusal of Prior's "Nut-brown Maid." How much he has surpassed Prior's work it is not necessary to mention, when perhaps it may be said, with justice, that he has excelled every composition of the same kind. The mixture of religious hope and resignation gives an elevation and dignity to disappointed love, which images merely natural cannot bestow. The gloom of a convent strikes the imagination with far greater force than the solitude of a grove. This piece was, however, not much his favourite in his later years, though I never heard upon what principle he slighted it.

In the next year (1713) he published "Windsor Forest," of which part was, as he relates, written at sixteen, about the same time as his Pastorals, and the latter part was added afterwards. Where the addition begins we are not told. The lines relating to the peace confess their own date. It is dedicated to Lord Lansdowne, who was then in high reputation and influence among the Tories; and it is said that the conclusion of the poem gave great pain to Addison, both as a poet and a politician. Reports like this are often spread with boldness very disproportionate to their evidence. Why should Addison receive any particular disturbance from the last lines of "Windsor Forest"? If contrariety of opinion could poison a politician, he could not live a day; and, as a poet, he must have felt Pope's force of genius much more from many other parts of his works. The pain that Addison might feel it is not likely that he would confess; and it is certain that he so well suppressed his discontent that Pope now thought himself his favourite, for, having been consulted in the revisal of "Cato" he introduced it by a prologue; and, when Dennis published his remarks, undertook, not indeed to vindicate, but to revenge his friend, by a "Narrative of the Frenzy of John Dennis."

There is reason to believe that Addison gave no encouragement to this disingenuous hostility, for, says Pope, in a letter to him, "indeed your opinion, that 'tis entirely to be neglected, would be my own in my own case; but I felt more warmth here than I did when I first saw his book against myself (though, indeed, in two minutes it made me heartily merry)." Addison was not a man on whom such cant of sensibility could make much impression. He left the pamphlet to itself, having disowned it to Dennis, and perhaps did not think Pope to have deserved much by his officiousness.

This year was printed in the Guardian the ironical comparison between the pastorals of Philips and Pope, a composition of artifice, criticism, and literature, to which nothing equal will easily be found. The superiority of Pope is so ingeniously dissembled, and the feeble lines of Philips so skilfully preferred, that Steele, being deceived, was unwilling to print the paper, lest Pope should be offended. Addison immediately saw the writer's design, and, as it seems, had malice enough to conceal his discovery, and to permit a publication which, by making his friend Philips ridiculous, made him for ever an enemy to Pope.

It appears that about this time Pope had a strong inclination to unite the art of painting with that of poetry, and put himself under the tuition of Jervas. He was near-sighted, and therefore not formed by nature for a painter; he tried, however, how far he could advance, and sometimes persuaded his friends to sit. A picture of Betterton, supposed to be drawn by him, was in the possession of Lord Mansfield. If this was taken from the life, he must have begun to paint earlier, for Betterton was now dead. Pope's ambition of this new art produced some encomiastic verses to Jervas, which certainly show his power as a poet; but I have been told that they betray his ignorance of painting. He appears to have regarded Betterton with kindness and esteem, and after his death published, under his name, a version into modern English of Chaucer's Prologues and one of his Tales, which, as was related by Mr. Harte, were believed to have been the performance of Pope himself by Fenton, who made him a gay offer of five pounds if he would show them in the hand of Betterton.

The next year (1713) produced a bolder attempt, by which profit was sought as well as praise. The poems which he had hitherto written, however they might have diffused his name, had made very little addition to his fortune. The allowance which his father made him, though, proportioned to what he had, it might be liberal, could not be large; his religion hindered him from the occupation of any civil employment; and he complained that he wanted even money to buy books. He therefore resolved to try how far the favour of the public extended by soliciting a subscription to a version of the "Iliad," with large notes. To print by subscription was, for some time, a practice peculiar to the English. The first considerable work for which this expedient was employed is said to have been Dryden's "Virgil," and it had been tried again with great success when the Tatlers were collected into volumes.

There was reason to believe that Pope's attempt would be successful. He was in the full bloom of reputation and was personally known to almost all whom dignity of employment or splendour of reputation had made eminent; he conversed indifferently with both parties, and never disturbed the public with his political opinions; and it might be naturally expected, as each faction then boasted its literary zeal, that the great men, who on other occasions practised all the violence of opposition, would emulate each other in their encouragement of a poet who delighted all, and by whom none had been offended. With these hopes, he offered an English "Iliad" to subscribers, in six volumes in quarto, for six guineas, a sum according to the value of money at that time by no means inconsiderable, and greater than I believe to have been ever asked before. His proposal, however, was very favourably received, and the patrons of literature were busy to recommend his undertaking and promote his interest. Lord Oxford, indeed, lamented that such a genius should be wasted upon a work not original, but proposed no means by which he might live without it. Addison recommended caution and moderation, and advised him not to be content with the praise of half the nation when he might be universally favoured.

The greatness of the design, the popularity of the author, and the attention of the literary world, naturally raised such expectations of the future sale, that the booksellers made their offers with great eagerness; but the highest bidder was Bernard Lintot, who became proprietor on condition of supplying, at his own expense, all the copies which were to be delivered to subscribers, or presented to friends, and paying two hundred pounds for every volume.

Of the quartos it was, I believe, stipulated that none should be printed but for the author, that the subscription might not be depreciated; but Lintot impressed the same pages upon a small folio, and paper perhaps a little thinner, and sold exactly at half the price, for half a guinea each volume, books so little inferior to the quartos that, by fraud of trade, those folios being afterwards shortened by cutting away the top and bottom, were sold as copies printed for the subscribers.

Lintot printed two hundred and fifty on royal paper in folio for two guineas a volume; of the small folio, having printed seventeen hundred and fifty copies of the first volume, he reduced the number in the other volumes to a thousand. It is unpleasant to relate that the bookseller, after all his hopes and all his liberality, was, by a very unjust and illegal action, defrauded of his profit. An edition of the English "Iliad" was printed in Holland in duodecimo, and imported clandestinely for the gratification of those who were impatient to read what they could not yet afford to buy. This fraud could only be counteracted by an edition equally cheap and more commodious; and Lintot was compelled to contract his folio at once into a duodecimo, and lose the advantage of an intermediate gradation. The notes which in the Dutch copies were placed at the end of each book as they had been in the large volumes, were now subjoined to the text in the same page, and are therefore more easily consulted. Of this edition two thousand five hundred were first printed, and five thousand a few weeks afterwards; but indeed great numbers were necessary to produce considerable profit.

Pope, having now emitted his proposals, and engaged not only his own reputation but in some degree that of his friends who patronised his subscription, began to be frightened at his own undertaking, and finding himself at first embarrassed with difficulties which retarded and oppressed him, he was for a time timorous and uneasy, had his nights disturbed by dreams of long journeys through unknown ways, and wished, as he said, "that somebody would hang him." This misery, however, was not of long continuance; he grew by degrees more acquainted with Homer's images and expressions, and practice increased his facility of versification. In a short time he represents himself as despatching regularly fifty verses a day, which would show him by an easy computation, the termination of his labour. His own diffidence was not his only vexation. He that asks a subscription soon finds that he has enemies. All who do not encourage him defame him. He that wants money would rather be thought angry than poor; and he that wishes to save his money conceals his avarice by his malice. Addison had hinted his suspicion that Pope was too much a Tory; and some of the Tories suspected his principles because he had contributed to the Guardian, which was carried on by Steele.

To those who censured his politics were added enemies more dangerous, who called in question his knowledge of Greek, and his qualifications for a translator of "Homer." To these he made no public opposition, but in one of his letters escapes from them as well as he can. At an age like his, for he was not more than twenty-five, with an irregular education and a course of life of which much seems to have passed in conversation, it is not very likely that he overflowed with Greek. But when he felt himself deficient he sought assistance, and what man of learning would refuse to help him? Minute inquiries into the force of words are less necessary in translating Homer than other poets, because his positions are general, and his representations natural, with very little dependence on local or temporary customs, on those changeable scenes of artificial life, which, by mingling original with accidental notions and crowding the mind with images which time effaces, produces ambiguity in dictation and obscurity in books. To this open display of unadulterated nature it must be ascribed that Homer has fewer passages of doubtful meaning than any other poet either in the learned or in modern languages. I have read of a man who, being by his ignorance of Greek compelled to gratify his curiosity with the Latin printed on the opposite page, declared that from the rude simplicity of the lines literally rendered he formed nobler ideas of the Homeric majesty than from the laboured elegance of polished versions. Those literal translations were always at hand, and from them he could easily obtain his author's sense with sufficient certainty and among the readers of Homer the number is very small of those who find much in the Greek more than in the Latin, except the music of the numbers.

If more help was wanting he had the poetical translation of Eobanus Hessus, an unwearied writer of Latin verses; he had the French Homers of La Valterie and Dacier, and the English of Chapman, Hobbes, and Ogilby. With Chapman, whose work, though now totally neglected, seems to have been popular almost to the end of the last century, he had very frequent consultations, and perhaps never translated any passage till he had read his version, which he indeed has been sometimes suspected of using instead of the original. Notes were likewise to be provided, for the six volumes would have been very little more than six pamphlets without them. What the mere perusal of the text could suggest Pope wanted no assistance to collect or methodise; but more was necessary. Many pages were to be filled, and learning must supply materials to wit and judgment. Something might be gathered from Dacier, but no man loves to be indebted to his contemporaries, and Dacier was accessible to common readers. Eustathius was therefore necessarily consulted. To read Eustathius, of whose work there was then no Latin version, I suspect Pope if he had been willing not to have been able. Some other was therefore to be found who had leisure as well as abilities, and he was doubtless most readily employed who would do much work for little money.

The history of the notes has never been traced. Broome, an his preface to his poems, declares himself the commentator "in part upon the 'Iliad,'" and it appears from Fenton's letter, preserved in the Museum, that Broome was at first engaged in consulting Eustathius; but that after a time, whatever was the reason, he desisted. Another man of Cambridge was then employed, who soon grew weary of the work, and a third, that was recommended by Thirlby, is now discovered to have been Jortin, a man since well known to the learned world, who complained that Pope, having accepted and approved his performance, never testified any curiosity to see him, and who professed to have forgotten the terms on which he worked. The terms which Fenton uses are very mercantile: "I think at first sight that his performance is very commendable, and have sent word for him to finish the seventeenth book, and to send it with his demands for his trouble. I have here enclosed the specimen; if the rest come before the return, I will keep them till I receive your order."

Broome then offered his service a second time, which was probably accepted, as they had afterwards a closer correspondence. Parnell contributed the "Life of Homer," which Pope found so harsh, that he took great pains in correcting it; and by his own diligence, with such help as kindness or money could procure him, in somewhat more than five years he completed his version of the "Iliad," with the notes. He began it in 1712, his twenty-fifth year, and concluded it in 1718, his thirtieth year. When we find him translating fifty lines a day, it is natural to suppose that he would have brought his work to a more speedy conclusion. The "Iliad," containing less than sixteen thousand verses, might have been despatched in less than three hundred and twenty days by fifty verses in a day. The notes, compiled with the assistance of his mercenaries, could not be supposed to require more time than the text. According to this calculation, the progress of Pope may seem to have been slow; but the distance is commonly very great between actual performances and speculative possibility. It is natural to suppose, that as much as has been done to-day may be done to-morrow; but on the morrow some difficulty emerges, or some external impediment obstructs.

Indolence, interruption, business, and pleasure, all take their turns of retardation; and every long work is lengthened by a thousand causes that can, and ten thousand that cannot, be recounted. Perhaps no extensive and multifarious performance was ever effected within the term originally fixed in the undertaker's mind. He that runs against time has an antagonist not subject to casualties.

The encouragement given to this translation, though report seems to have overrated it, was such as the world has not often seen. The subscribers were five hundred and seventy-five. The copies, for which subscriptions were given, were six hundred and fifty-four; and only six hundred and sixty were printed. For these copies Pope had nothing to pay. He therefore received, including the two hundred pounds a volume, five thousand three hundred and twenty pounds, four shillings, without deduction, as the books were supplied by Lintot.

By the success of his subscription Pope was relieved from those pecuniary distresses with which, notwithstanding his popularity, he had hitherto struggled. Lord Oxford had often lamented his disqualification for public employment, but never proposed a pension. While the translation of "Homer" was in its progress, Mr. Craggs, then Secretary of State, offered to procure him a pension, which, at least during his ministry, might be enjoyed with secrecy. This was not accepted by Pope, who told him, however, that, if he should be pressed with want of money, he would send to him for occasional supplies. Craggs was not long in power, and was never solicited for money by Pope, who disdained to beg what he did not want.

With the product of this subscription, which he had too much discretion to squander, he secured his future life from want, by considerable annuities. The estate of the Duke of Buckingham was found to have been charged with five hundred pounds a year, payable to Pope, which doubtless his translation enabled him to purchase.

It cannot be unwelcome to literary curiosity, that I deduce thus minutely the history of the English "Iliad." It is certainly the noblest version of poetry which the world has ever seen, and its publication must therefore be considered as one of the great events in the annals of learning. To those who have skill to estimate the excellence and difficulty of this great work, it must be very desirable to know how it was performed, and by what gradations it advanced to correctness. Of such an intellectual process the knowledge has very rarely been attainable; but happily there remains the original copy of the "Iliad," which, being obtained by Bolingbroke as a curiosity, descended from him to Mallet, and is now, by the solicitation of the late Dr. Maty, reposited in the Museum. Between this manuscript, which is written upon accidental fragments of paper, and the printed edition, there must have been an intermediate copy, that was perhaps destroyed as it returned from the press.

From the first copy I have procured a few transcripts, and shall exhibit first the printed lines; then, in a small print, those of the manuscripts, with all their variations. Those words in the small print, which are given in italics, are cancelled in the copy, and the words placed under them adopted in their stead:

The beginning of the first book stands thus:-

   The wrath of Peleus' son, the direful spring Of all the Grecian woes, O Goddess, sing, That wrath which hurled to Pluto's gloomy reign The souls of mighty chiefs untimely slain.

The stern Pelides' rage, O Goddess, sing,
wrath

Of all the woes of Greece too fatal spring,
Grecian
That screwed with warriors dead the Phrygian plain,
heroes
And peopled the dark with heroes slain:
filled the shady hell with chiefs untimely
Whose limbs, unburied on the naked shore, Devouring dogs and hungry vultures tore, Since great Achilles and Atrides strove; Such was the sovereign doom, and such the will of Jove.

Whose limbs, unburied on the hostile shore,
Devouring dogs and greedy vultures tore,
Since first Atrides and Achilles strove;
Such was the sovereign doom, and such the will of Jove.
Declare, O Muse, in what ill-fated hour Sprung the fierce strife from what offended Power? Latona's son a dire contagion spread, And heaped the camp with mountains of the dead;
The King of Men his reverend priest defied, And for the King's offence the people died.

Declare, O Goddess, what offended Power
Enflamed their rage in that ill-omened hour;
anger fatal, hapless
Phoebus himself the dire debate procured,
fierce
To avenge the wrongs his injured priest endured;
For this the god a dire infection spread,
And heaped the camp with millions of the dead:
The King of men the sacred sire defied,
And for the King's offence the people died.
For Chryses sought with costly gifts to gain His captive daughter from the Victor's chain; Suppliant the venerable father stands, Apollo's awful ensigns grace his hands, By these he begs, and, lowly bending down, Extends the sceptre and the

laurel crown.

> For Chryses sought by presents to regain
> costly gifts to gain
> His captive daughter from the Victor's chain;
> Suppliant the venerable father stands,
> Apollo's awful ensigns graced his hands.
> By these he begs, and, lowly bending down
> The golden sceptre and the laurel crown,
> Presents the sceptre
> For these as ensigns of his god he bare,
> The god who sends his golden shaft afar;
> Then low on earth the venerable man,
> Suppliant before the brother kings began.

He sued to all, but chief implored for grace, The brother kings of Atreus' royal race; Ye kings and warriors, may your vows be crowned, And Troy's proud walls lie level with the ground; May Jove restore you, when your toils are o'er, Safe to the pleasures of your native shore.

> To all he sued, but chief implored for grace
> The brother kings of Atreus' royal race.
> Ye sons of Atreus, may your vows be crowned,
> kings and warriors
> Your labours, by the gods be all your labours crowned;
> So may the gods your arms with conquest bless,
> And Troy's proud walls lie level with the ground;
> Till laid
> And crown your labours with desired success;
> May Jove restore you when your toils are o'er
> Safe to the pleasures of your native shore.

But, oh! relieve a wretched parent's pain, And give Chryses to these arms again; If mercy fail, yet let my present move, And dread avenging Phoebus, son of Jove.

But, oh! relieve a hapless parent's pain,
And give my daughter to these arms again;
Receive my gifts, if mercy fails, yet let my present move,
And fear the god who deals his darts around,
avenging Phoebus, son of Jove.
The Greeks, in shouts, their joint assent declare, The priest to reverence, and release the fair: Not so Atrides; he, with kingly pride, Repulsed the sacred sire, and thus replied.

He said, the Greeks their joint assent declare,
The father said, the generous Greeks relent,
To accept the ransom, and restore the fair:
Revere the priest, and speak their joint assent;
Not so the tyrant; he, with kingly pride,
Atrides,
Repulsed the sacred sire, and thus replied
[Not so the tyrant. DRYDEN.]

Of these lines, and of the whole first book, I am told that there was yet a former copy, more varied, and more deformed with interlineations.

The beginning of the second book varies very little from the printed page, and is therefore set down without any parallel. The few slight differences do not require to be elaborately displayed.

Now pleasing sleep had sealed each mortal eye: Stretched in the tents the Grecian leaders lie; The Immortals slumbered on their thrones above, All but the ever-wakeful eye of Jove. To honour Thetis' son he bends his care, And plunge the Greeks in all the woes of war. Then bids an empty phantom rise to sight, And thus commands the vision of the night:

directs Fly hence, delusive dream, and, light as air, To Agamemnon's royal tent repair; Bid him in arms draw forth the embattled train, March all his legions to the dusty plain. Now tell the King 'tis given him to destroy Declare even now The lofty walls of wide-extended Troy;

    towers For now no more the gods with fate contend; At Juno's suit the heavenly factions end. Destruction hovers o'er yon devoted wall,

    hangs And nodding Ilion waits the impending fall.

    Invocation to the catalogue of ships.

    Say, virgins, seated round the throne divine, All-knowing goddesses! immortal nine! Since earth's wide regions, heaven's unmeasured height, And hell's abyss, hide nothing from your sight (We, wretched mortals! lost in doubts below, But guess by rumour, and but boast we know), Oh! say what heroes, fired by thirst of fame, Or urged by wrongs, to Troy's destruction came! To count them all demands a thousand tongues, A throat of brass and adamantine lungs.

    Now virgin goddesses, immortal nine!
    That round Olympus' heavenly summit shine,
    Who see through heaven and earth, and hell profound,
    And all things know, and all things can resound!
    Relate what armies sought the Trojan land,
    What nations followed, and what chiefs command;
    (For doubtful fame distracts mankind below,
    And nothing can we tell, and nothing know)

    Without your aid, to count the unnumbered train, A thousand mouths, a thousand tongues, were vain.

    Book V. v. 1.

    But Pallas now Tydides' soul inspires, Fills with her force, and warms with all her fires: Above the Greeks his deathless fame to raise, And crown her hero with distinguished praise, High on his helm celestial lightnings play, His beamy shield emits a living ray; The unwearied blaze incessant streams supplies, Like the red star that fires the autumnal skies.

    But Pallas now Tydides' soul inspires, Fills with her rage, and warms with all her fires;

    force O'er all the Greeks decrees his fame to raise, Above the Greeks her warrior's fame to raise, his deathless And crown her hero with immortal praise:

distinguished Bright from his beamy crest the lightnings play,

High on helm From his broad buckler flashed the living ray; High on his helm celestial lightnings play, His beamy shield emits a living ray; The goddess with her breath the flame supplies, Bright as the star whose fires in autumn rise; Her breath divine thick streaming flames supplies, Bright as the star that fires the autumnal skies: The unwearied blaze incessant streams supplies, Like the red star that fires the autumnal skies.

When fresh he rears his radiant orb to sight, And bathed in ocean shoots a keener light, Such glories Pallas on the chief bestowed, Such from his arms the fierce effulgence flowed; Onward she drives him, furious to engage, Where the fight burns, and where the thickest rage.

> When fresh he rears his radiant orb to sight,
> And gilds old ocean with a blaze of light,
> Bright as the star that fires the autumnal skies,
> Fresh from the deep, and gilds the seas and skies:
> Such glories Pallas on her chief bestowed,
> Such sparkling rays from his bright armour flowed,
> Such sparkling rays from his bright armour flowed,
> Onward she drives him headlong to engage,
> furious
> Where the war bleeds, and where the fiercest rage.
> fight burns, thickest

The sons of Dares first the combat sought, A wealthy priest, but rich without a fault; In Vulcan's fane the father's days were led, The sons to toils of glorious battle bred;

> There lived a Trojan--Dares was his name,
> The priest of Vulcan, rich, yet void of blame;
> The sons of Dares first the combat sought,
> A wealthy priest, but rich without a fault.
> Conclusion of Book VIII. v. 687.

As when the moon, refulgent lamp of night, O'er heaven's clear azure spreads her sacred light, When not a breath disturbs the deep serene, And not a cloud o'ercasts the solemn scene; Around her throne the vivid planets roll, And stars unnumbered gild the glowing pole: O'er the dark trees a yellower verdure shed, And tip with silver every mountain's head: Then shine the vales--the rocks in prospect rise, A flood of glory bursts from all the skies; The conscious swains, rejoicing in the sight, Eye the blue vault, and bless the useful light. So many flames before proud Ilion blaze, And lighten glimmering Xanthus with their rays; The long reflections of the distant fires Gleam on the walls, and tremble on the spires. A thousand piles the dusky horrors gild, And shoot a shady lustre o'er the field; Full fifty guards each flaming pile attend, Whose umbered arms by fits thick flashes send; Loud neigh the coursers o'er their heaps of corn, And ardent warriors wait the rising morn.

As when in stillness of the silent night,
As when the moon in all her lustre bright,
As when the moon, refulgent lamp of night,
O'er Heaven's clear azure sheds her silver light;
pure spreads sacred
As still in air the trembling lustre stood,
And o'er its golden border shoots a flood;
When no loose gale disturbs the deep serene,
not a breath
And no dim cloud o'ercasts the solemn scene;
not a
Around her silver throne the planets glow,
And stars unnumbered trembling beams bestow;
Around her throne the vivid planets roll,
And stars unnumbered gild the glowing pole:
Clear gleams of light o'er the dark trees are seen,
o'er the dark trees a yellow sheds
O'er the dark trees a yellower green they shed,
gleam
verdure

And tip with silver all the mountain heads
forest
And tip with silver every mountain's head.
The valleys open, and the forests rise,
The vales appear, the rocks in prospect rise,
Then shine the vales, the rocks in prospect rise,
All nature stands revealed before our eyes;
A flood of glory bursts from all the skies.
The conscious shepherd, joyful at the sight,
Eyes the blue vault, and numbers every light.
The conscious swains rejoicing at the sight,
shepherds gazing with delight
Eye the blue vault, and bless the vivid light.
glorious
useful
So many flames before the navy blaze,
proud Ilion
And lighten glimmering Xanthus with their rays,
Wide o'er the fields to Troy extend the gleams,
And tip the distant spires with fainter beams;
The long reflections of the distant fires
Gild the high walls, and tremble on the spires;
Gleam on the walls, and tremble on the spires;
A thousand fires at distant stations bright,
Gild the dark prospect, and dispel the night.

Of these specimens every man who has cultivated poetry, or who delights to trace the mind from the rudeness of its first conceptions to the elegance of its last, will naturally desire a great number; but most other readers are already tired, and I am not writing only to poets and philosophers.

The "Iliad" was published volume by volume, as the translation proceeded. The four first books appeared in 1713. The expectation of this work was undoubtedly high, and every man who had connected his name with criticism or poetry was desirous of such intelligence as might enable him to talk upon the popular topic. Halifax, who, by having been first a poet, and then a patron of poetry, had acquired the right of being a judge, was willing to hear some books while they were yet un-published. Of this rehearsal Pope afterwards gave the following account:-

"The famous Lord Halifax was rather a pretender to taste than really possessed of it. When I had finished the two or three first books of my translation of the 'Iliad,' that lord desired to have the pleasure of hearing them read at his house. Addison, Congreve, and Garth were there at the reading. In four or five places Lord Halifax stopped me very civilly, and with a speech each time of much the same kind, 'I beg your pardon, Mr. Pope, but there is something in that passage that does not please me. Be so good as to mark the place, and consider it a little at your leisure. I am sure you can give it a little turn.' I returned from Lord Halifax's with Dr. Garth in his chariot, and as we were going along was saying to the Doctor that my lord had laid me under a great deal of difficulty by such loose and general observations; that I had been thinking over the passages almost ever since, and could not guess at what it was that offended his lordship in either of them. Garth laughed heartily at my embarrassment: said I had not been long enough acquainted with Lord Halifax to know his way yet; that I need not puzzle myself about looking those places over and over when I got home. 'All you need do,' says he, 'is to leave them just as they are, call on Lord Halifax two or three months hence, thank him for his kind ob-servations on those passages, and then read them to him as altered. I have known him much longer than you have, and will be answerable for the event.' I followed his advice, waited on Lord Halifax some time after; said I hoped he would find his objections to those passages removed; read them to him exactly as they were at first; and his lordship was extremely pleased with them, and cried out, 'Ay, now they are perfectly right; nothing can be better.'"

It is seldom that the great or the wise suspect that they are despised or cheated. Halifax, thinking this a lucky opportunity of securing immortality, made some ad-vances of favour and some overtures of advantage to Pope, which he seems to have received with sullen coldness. All our knowledge of this transaction is derived from a single letter (December 1, 1714), in which Pope says, "I am obliged to you, both for the favours you have done me and those you intend me. I distrust neither your will nor your memory when it is to do good; and if I ever become troublesome or solicitous, it must not be out of expectation, but out of gratitude. Your lordship may cause me to live agreeably in the town, or contentedly in the country, which is really all the difference I set between an easy fortune and a small one. It is indeed a high strain of generosity in you to think of making me easy all my life, only because I have been so happy as to divert you some few hours; but, if I may have leave to add it is because you think me no enemy to my native country, there will appear a better reason; for I must of consequence be very much (as I sincerely am) yours, &c."

These voluntary offers, and this faint acceptance, ended without effect. The patron was not accustomed to such frigid gratitude; and the poet fed his own pride with the dignity of independence. They probably were suspicious of each other. Pope would not dedicate till he saw at what rate his praise was valued; he would be "troublesome out of gratitude, not expectation." Halifax thought himself entitled to confidence, and would give nothing unless he knew what he should receive. Their commerce had its beginning in hope of praise on one side and of money on the other, and ended because Pope was less eager of money than Halifax of praise. It is not likely that Halifax had any personal benevolence to Pope; it is evident that Pope looked on Halifax with scorn and hatred.

The reputation of this great work failed of gaining him a patron but it deprived him of a friend. Addison and he were now at the head of poetry and criticism, and both in such a state of elevation that, like the two rivals in the Roman State, one could no longer bear an equal, nor the other a superior. Of the gradual abatement of kindness between friends, the beginning is often scarcely discernible to themselves, and the process is continued by petty provocations, and incivilities sometimes peevishly returned, and sometimes contemptuously neglected, which would escape all attention but that of pride, and drop from any memory but that of resentment. That the quarrel of these two wits should be minutely deduced is not to be expected from a writer to whom, as Homer says, "nothing but rumour has reached, and who has no personal knowledge."

Pope doubtless approached Addison, when the reputation of their wit first brought them together, with the respect due to a man whose abilities were acknowledged, and who, having attained that eminence to which he was himself aspiring, had in his hands the distribution of literary fame. He paid court with sufficient diligence by his prologue to "Cato," by his abuse of Dennis, and with praise yet more direct, by his poem on the "Dialogues on Medals," of which the immediate publication was then intended. In all this there was no hypocrisy for he confessed that he found in Addison something more pleasing than in any other man.

It may be supposed that, as Pope saw himself favoured by the world, and more frequently compared his own powers with those of others, his confidence increased, and his submission lessened; and that Addison felt no delight from the advances of a young wit, who might soon contend with him for the highest place. Every great man, of whatever kind be his greatness, has among his friends those who officiously or insidiously quicken his attention to offences, heighten his disgust, and stimulate his resentment. Of such adherents Addison doubtless had many; and Pope was now too high to be without them. From the emission and reception of the proposals for the "Iliad," the kindness of Addison seems to have abated. Jervas the painter once pleased himself (August 20,1714) with imagining that he had re-established their friendship, and wrote to Pope that Addison once suspected him of too close a confederacy with Swift, but was now satisfied with his conduct. To this Pope answered, a week after, that his engagements to Swift were such as his services in regard to the subscription demanded, and that the Tories never put him under the necessity of asking leave to be grateful. "But," says he, "as Mr. Addison must be the judge in what regards himself, and seems to have no very just one in regard to me, so I must own to you I expect nothing but civility from him." In the same letter he mentions Philips, as having been busy to kindle animosity between them; but in a letter to Addison he expresses some consciousness of behaviour, inattentively deficient in respect.

Of Swift's industry in promoting the subscription there remains the testimony of Kennet, no friend to either him or Pope.

"November 2, 1713, Dr. Swift came into the coffee-house, and had a bow from everybody but me, who, I confess, could not but despise him. When I came to the antechamber to wait, before prayers, Dr. Swift was the principal man of talk and business, and acted as master of requests. Then he instructed a young nobleman that the BEST POET IN ENGLAND was Mr. Pope (a papist), who had begun a translation of 'Homer' into English verse, for which HE MUST HAVE THEM ALL SUBSCRIBE: for, says he, the author SHALL NOT begin to print till *I* HAVE a thousand guineas for him."

About this time it is likely that Steele, who was, with all his political fury, good-natured and officious, procured an interview between these angry rivals, which ended in aggravated malevolence. On this occasion, if the reports be true, Pope made his complaint with frankness and spirit, as a man undeservedly neglected or opposed; and Addison affected a contemptuous unconcern, and in a calm, even voice reproached Pope with his vanity, and, telling him of the improvements which his early works had received from his own remarks and those of Steele, said that he, being now engaged in public business, had no longer any care for his poetical reputation, nor had any other desire with regard to Pope than that he should not, by too much arrogance, alienate the public.

To this Pope is said to have replied with great keenness and severity, upbraiding Addison with perpetual dependence, and with the abuse of those qualifications which he had obtained at the public cost, and charging him with mean endeavours to obstruct the progress of rising merit. The contest rose so high that they parted at last without any interchange of civility.

The first volume of "Homer" was (1715) in time published; and a rival version of the first "Iliad," for rivals the time of their appearance inevitably made them, was immediately printed, with the name of Tickell. It was soon perceived that, among the followers of Addison, Tickell had the preference, and the critics and poets divided into factions. "I," says Pope, "have the town, that is, the mob, on my side; but it is not uncommon for the smaller party to supply by industry what it wants in numbers. I appeal to the people as my rightful judges, and, while they are not inclined to condemn me, shall not fear the high-flyers at Button's." This opposition he immediately imputed to Addison, and complained of it in terms sufficiently resentful to Craggs, their common friend.

When Addison's opinion was asked, he declared the versions to be both good, but Tickell's the best that had ever been written; and sometimes said that they were both good, but that Tickell had more of "Homer."

Pope was now sufficiently irritated; his reputation and his interest were at hazard. He once intended to print together the four versions of Dryden, Maynwaring, Pope, and Tickell, that they might be readily compared and fairly estimated. This design seems to have been defeated by the refusal off Tonson, who was the proprietor of the other three versions.

Pope intended, at another time, a rigorous criticism of Tickell's translation, and had marked a copy, which I have seen, in all places that appeared defective. But while he was thus meditating defence or revenge, his adversary sunk before him without a blow; the voice of the public was not long divided, and the preference universally given to Pope's performance. He was convinced, by adding one circumstance to another, that the other translation was the work of Addison himself; but, if he knew it in Addison's lifetime, it does not appear that he told it. He left his illustrious antagonist to lie punished by what has been considered as the most painful of all reflections--the remembrance of a crime perpetrated in vain. The other circumstances of their quarrel were thus related by Pope:-

"Philips seemed to have been encouraged to abuse me in coffee-houses and conversations, and Gildon wrote a thing about Wycherley, in which he had abused both me and my relations very grossly. Lord Warwick himself told me one day that it was in vain for me to endeavour to be well with Mr. Addison; that his jealous temper would never admit of a settled friendship between us; and, to convince me of what he had said, assured me that Addison had encouraged Gildon to publish those scandals, and had given him ten guineas after they were published. The next day, while I was heated with what I had heard, I wrote a letter to Mr. Addison, to let him know that I was not unacquainted with this behaviour of his; that if I was to speak severely of him in return for it, it should not be in such a dirty way; that I should rather tell him himself fairly of his faults, and allow his good qualities; and that it should be something in the following manner. I then adjoined the first sketch of what has since been called my satire on Addison. Mr Addison used me very civilly ever after."

The verses on Addison, when they were sent to Atterbury, were considered by him as the most excellent of Pope's performances; and the writer was advised, since he knew where his strength lay, not to suffer it to remain unemployed. This year (1715), being by the subscription enabled to live more by choice, having persuaded his father to sell their estate at Binfield, he purchased, I think only for his life, that house at Twickenham to which his residence afterwards procured so much celebration, and removed thither with his father and mother. Here he planted the vines and the quincunx which his verses mention; and being under the necessity of making a subterraneous passage to a garden on the other side of the road, he adorned it with fossil bodies, and dignified it with the title of a grotto; a place of silence and retreat, from which he endeavoured to persuade his friends and himself that cares and passions could be excluded.

A grotto is not often the wish or pleasure of all Englishmen, who has more frequent need to solicit than exclude the sun; but Pope's excavation was requisite as an entrance to his garden; and, as some men try to be proud of their defects, he extracted an ornament from an inconvenience, and vanity produced a grotto where necessity enforced a passage. It may be frequently remarked of the studious and speculative, that they are proud of trifles, and that their amusements seem frivolous and childish. Whether it be that men, conscious of great reputation, think themselves above the reach of censure, and safe in the admission of negligent indulgences, or that mankind expect from elevated genius a uniformity of greatness, and watch its degradation with malicious wonder, like him who, having followed with his eye an eagle into the clouds, should lament that she ever descended to a perch.

While the volumes of his "Homer" were annually published, he collected his former works (1717) into one quarto volume, to which he prefixed a preface, written with great sprightliness and elegance, which was afterwards reprinted, with some passages subjoined that he at first omitted. Other marginal additions of the same kind he made in the later editions of his poems. Waller remarks, that poets lose half their praise, because the reader knows not what they have blotted. Pope's voracity of fame taught him the art of obtaining the accumulated honour both of what he had published, and of what he had suppressed. In this year his father died suddenly, in his seventy-fifth year, having passed twenty-nine years in privacy. He is not known but by the character which his son has given him. If the money with which he retired was all gotten by himself, he had traded very successfully in times when sudden riches were rarely attainable.

The publication of the "Iliad" was at last completed in 1720. The splendour and success of this work raised Pope many enemies that endeavoured to depreciate his abilities. Burnet, who was afterwards a judge of no mean reputation, censured him in a piece called "Homerides" before it was published. Ducket likewise endeavoured to make him ridiculous. Dennis was the perpetual persecutor of all his studies. But whoever his critics were, their writings are lost, and the names, which are preserved are preserved in the "Dunciad."

In this disastrous year (1720) of national infatuation, when more riches than Peru can boast were expected from the South Sea, when the contagion of avarice tainted every mind, and even poets panted after wealth, Pope was seized with the universal passion, and ventured some of his money. The stock rose in its price, and for a while he thought himself the lord of thousands. But this dream of happiness did not last long, and he seems to have waked soon enough to get clear with the loss of what he once thought himself to have won, and perhaps not wholly of that.

Next year he published some select poems of his friend Dr. Parnell, with a very elegant dedication to the Earl of Oxford, who, after all his struggles and dangers, then lived in retirement, still under the frown of a victorious faction, who could take no pleasure in hearing his praise. He gave the same year (1721) an edition of Shakespeare. His name was now of so much authority that Tonson thought himself entitled, by annexing it, to demand a subscription of six guineas for Shakespeare's plays in six quarto volumes. Nor did his expectation much deceive him, for, of seven hundred and fifty which he printed, he dispersed a great number at the price proposed. The reputation of that edition indeed, sunk, afterwards so low, that one hundred and forty copies were sold at sixteen shillings each. On this undertaking, to which Pope was induced by a reward of two hundred and seventeen pounds twelve shillings, he seems never to have reflected afterwards without vexation; for Theobald a man of heavy diligence, with very slender powers, first, in a book called "Shakespeare Restored," and then in a formal edition, detected his deficiencies with all the insolence of victory; and as he was now high enough to be feared and hated, Theobald had from others all the help that could be supplied, by the desire of humbling a haughty character. From this time Pope became an enemy to editors, collators, commentators, and verbal critics, and hoped to persuade the world that he miscarried in this undertaking only by having a mind too great for such minute employment.

Pope in his edition undoubtedly did many things wrong, and left many things undone; but let him not be defrauded of his due praise. He was the first that knew, at least the first that told, by what helps the text might be improved. If he inspected the early editions negligently, he taught others to be more accurate. In his preface he expanded with great skill and elegance the character which had been given of Shakespeare by Dryden; and he drew the public attention upon his works, which, though often mentioned, had been little read. Soon after the appearance of the "Iliad," resolving not to let the general kindness cool, he published proposals for a translation of the "Odyssey," in five volumes, for five guineas. He was willing, however, now to have associates in his labour, being either weary with toiling upon another's thoughts, or having heard, as Ruffhead relates, that Fenton and Broome had already begun the work, and liking better to have them confederates than rivals. In the patent, instead of saying that he had "translated" the "Odyssey," as he had said of the "Iliad," he says that he had "undertaken" a translation: and in the proposals, the subscription is said to be not solely for his own use, but for that of "two of his friends who have assisted him in his work."

In 1723, while he was engaged in this new version, he appeared before the Lords at the memorable trial of Bishop Atterbury, with whom he had lived in great familiarity, and frequent correspondence. Atterbury had honestly recommended to him the study of the Popish controversy, in hope of his conversion; to which Pope answered in a manner that cannot much recommend his principles or his judgment. In questions and projects of learning they agree better. He was called at the trial to give an account of Atterbury's domestic life and private employment, that it might appear how little time he had left for plots. Pope had but few words to utter, and in those few he made several blunders.

His letters to Atterbury express the utmost esteem, tenderness, and gratitude. "Perhaps," says he, "it is not only in this world that I may have cause to remember the Bishop of Rochester." At their last interview in the Tower, Atterbury presented him with a Bible.

Of the "Odyssey" Pope translated only twelve books. The rest were the work of Broome and Fenton: the notes were written wholly by Broome, who was not over liberally rewarded. The public was carefully kept ignorant of the several shares; and an account was subjoined at the conclusion which is now known not to be true. The first copy of Pope's books, with those of Fenton, are to be seen in the Museum. The parts of Pope are less interlined than the "Iliad," and the latter books of the "Iliad" less than the former. He grew dexterous by practice, and every sheet enabled him to write the next with more facility. The books of Fenton have very few alterations by the hand of Pope. Those of Broome have not been found, but Pope complained, as it is reported, that he had much trouble in correcting them. His contract with Lintot was the same as for the "Iliad," except that only one hundred pounds were to be paid him for each volume. The number of subscribers were five hundred and seventy-four, and of copies eight hundred and nineteen, so that his profit, when he had paid his assistants, was still very considerable. The work was finished in 1723; and from that time he resolved to make no more translations. The sale did not answer Lintot's expectation, and he then pretended to discover something of a fraud in Pope, and commenced or threatened a suit in Chancery.

On the English "Odyssey" a criticism was published by Spence, at that time Prelector of Poetry at Oxford, a man whose learning was not very great, and whose mind was not very powerful. His criticism, however, was commonly just; what he thought he thought rightly, and his remarks were recommended by his coolness and candour. In him Pope had the first experience of a critic without malevolence, who thought it as much his duty to display beauties as expose faults, who censured with respect, and praised with alacrity. With this criticism Pope was so little offended, that he sought the acquaintance of the writer, who lived with him from that time in great familiarity, attended him in his last hours, and compiled memorials of his conversation. The regard of Pope recommended him to the great and powerful, and he obtained very valuable preferments in the Church. Not long after Pope was returning home from a visit in a friend's coach, which, in passing a bridge, was overturned into the water; the window's were closed, and, being unable to force them open, he was in danger of immediate death, when the postillion snatched him out by breaking the glass, of which the fragments cut two of his fingers in such a manner that he lost their use.

Voltaire, who was then in England, sent him a letter of consolation. He had been entertained by Pope at his table, where he talked with so much grossness that Mrs. Pope was driven from the room. Pope discovered, by a trick, that he was a spy for the Court, and never considered him as a man worthy of confidence. He soon afterwards (1727) joined with Swift, who was then in England, to publish three volumes of "Miscellanies," in which, amongst other things, he inserted the "Memoirs of a Parish Clerk," in ridicule of Burnet's importance in his own history, and a "Debate upon Black and White Horses," written in all the formalities of a legal process by the assistance, as is said, of Mr. Fortescue, afterwards Master of the Rolls. Before these "Miscellanies" is a preface signed by Swift and Pope, but apparently written by Pope, in which he makes a ridiculous and romantic complaint of the robberies committed upon authors by the clandestine seizure and sale of their papers. He tells in tragic strains how "the cabinets of the sick and the closets of the dead have been broken open and ransacked," as if those violences were often committed for papers of uncertain and accidental value which are rarely provoked by real treasures--as if epigrams and essays were in danger where gold and diamonds are safe. A cat hunted for his musk is, according to Pope's account, but the emblem of a wit winded by booksellers. His complaint, however, received some attestation, for the same year the letters written by him to Mr. Cromwell in his youth were sold by Mrs. Thomas to Curll, who printed them.

In these "Miscellanies" was first published the "Art of Sinking in Poetry," which, by such a train of consequences as usually passes in literary quarrels, gave in a short time, according to Pope's account, occasion to the "Dunciad."

In the following year (1728) he began to put Atterbury's advice in practice, and showed his satirical powers by publishing the "Dunciad," one of his greatest and most elaborate performances, in which he endeavoured to sink into contempt all the writers by whom he had been attacked, and some others whom he thought unable to defend themselves. At the head of the "Dunces" he placed poor Theobald, whom he accused of ingratitude, but whose real crime was supposed to be that of having revised Shakespeare more happily than himself. This satire had the effect which he intended, by blasting the characters which it touched. Ralph, who, unnecessarily interposing in the quarrel, got a place in a subsequent edition, complained that for a time he was in danger of starving, as the booksellers had no longer any confidence in his capacity. The prevalence of this poem was gradual and slow: the plan, if not wholly new, was little understood by common readers. Many of the allusions required illustration; the names were often expressed only by the initial and final letters, and if they had been printed at length were such as few had known or recollected. The subject itself had nothing generally interesting, for whom did it concern to know that one or another scribbler was a dunce? If, therefore, it had been possible for those who were attacked to conceal their pain and their resentment, the "Dunciad" might have made its way very slowly in the world. This, however, was not to be expected: every man is of importance to himself, and therefore, in his own opinion, to others; and, supposing the world already acquainted with all his pleasures and his pains, is perhaps the first to publish injuries or misfortunes, which had never been known unless related by himself, and at which those that hear them will only laugh, for no man sympathises with the sorrows of vanity.

The history of the "Dunciad" is very minutely related by Pope himself in a dedication which he wrote to Lord Middlesex in the name of Savage.

"I will relate the war of the 'Dunces' (for so it has been commonly called), which began in the year 1727, and ended in 1730

"When Dr. Swift and Mr. Pope thought it proper, for reasons specified in the preface to their 'Miscellanies,' to publish such little pieces of theirs as had occasionally got abroad, there was added to them the 'Treatise of the Bathos, or the Art of Sinking in Poetry.' It happened that in one chapter of this piece the several species of bad poets were ranged in classes, to which were prefixed almost all the letters of the alphabet (the greatest part of them at random); but such was the number of poets eminent in that art, that some one or other took every letter to himself. All fell into so violent a fury, that, for half a year or more, the common newspapers (in most of which they had some property, as being hired writers) were filled with the most abusive falsehoods and scurrilities they could possibly devise, a liberty no way to be wondered at in those people, and in those papers, that, for many years during the uncontrolled license of the Press, had aspersed almost all the great characters of the age; and this with impunity, their own persons and names being utterly secret and obscure. This gave Mr. Pope the thought that he had now some opportunity of doing good by detecting and dragging into light these common enemies of mankind, since, to invalidate this universal slander, it sufficed to show what contemptible men were the authors of it. He was not without hopes that, by manifesting the dulness of those who had only malice to recommend them, either the booksellers would not find their account in employing them, or the men themselves, when discovered, want courage to proceed in so unlawful an occupation. This it was that gave birth to the 'Dunciad,' and he thought it a happiness that, by the late flood of slander on himself, he had acquired such a peculiar right over their names as was necessary to this design.

"On the 12th of March, 1729, at St. James's, that poem was presented to the king and queen (who had before been pleased to read it) by the Right Honourable Sir Robert Walpole, and some days after the whole impression was taken and dispersed by several noblemen and persons of the first distinction.

It is certainly a true observation that no people are so impatient of censure as those who are the greatest slanderers, which was wonderfully exemplified on this occasion. On the day the book was first vended a crowd of authors besieged the shop; entreaties, advices, threats of law and battery--nay, cries of treason--were all employed to hinder the coming out of the 'Dunciad.' On the other side, the booksellers and hawkers made as great efforts to procure it. What could a few poor authors do against so great a majority as the public? There was no stopping a torrent with a finger, so out it came.

"Many ludicrous circumstances attended it. The 'Dunces' (for by this name they were called) held weekly clubs, to consult of hostilities against the author. One wrote a letter to a great minister, assuring him Mr. Pope was the greatest enemy the Government had, and another bought his image in clay to execute him in effigy, with which sad sort of satisfaction the gentlemen were a little comforted. Some false editions of the book, having an owl in their frontispiece, the true one, to distinguish it, fixed in his stead an ass laden with authors. Then another surreptitious one being printed with the same ass, the new edition in octavo returned for distinction to the owl again. Hence arose a great contest of booksellers against booksellers, and advertisements against advertisements, some recommending the edition of the owl, and others the edition of the ass, by which names they came to be distinguished, to the great honour also of the gentlemen of the 'Dunciad.'"

Pope appears by this narrative to have contemplated his victory over the "Dunces" with great exultation; and such was his delight in the tumult which he had raised, that for a while his natural sensibility was suspended, and he read reproaches and invectives without emotion, considering them only as the necessary effects of that pain which he rejoiced in having given. It cannot, however, be concealed that, by his own confession, he was the aggressor, for nobody believes that the letters in the "Bathos" were placed at random; and at may be discovered that, when he thinks himself concealed, he indulges the common vanity of common men, and triumphs in those distinctions which he affected to despise. He is proud that his book was presented to the king and queen by the Right Honourable Sir Robert Walpole; he is proud that they had read it before; he is proud that the edition was taken off by the nobility and persons of the first distinction. The edition of which he speaks was, I believe, that which, by telling in the text the names, and in the notes the characters, of those whom he had satirised, was made intelligible and diverting. The critics had now declared their approbation of the plan, and the common reader began to like it without fear. Those who were strangers to petty literature, and therefore unable to decipher initials and blanks, had now names and persons brought within their view, and delighted in the visible effects of those shafts of malice which they had hitherto contemplated as shot into the air.

Dennis, upon the fresh provocation now given him, renewed the enmity which had for a time been appeased by mutual civilities, and published remarks, which he had till then suppressed, upon the "Rape of the Lock." Many more grumbled in secret, or vented their resentment in the newspapers by epigrams or invectives. Ducket, indeed, being mentioned as loving Burnet with "pious passion," pretended that his moral character was injured, and for some time declared his resolution to take vengeance with a cudgel. But Pope appeased him, by changing "pious passion" to "cordial friendship," and by a note, in which he vehemently disclaims the malignity of the meaning imputed to the first expression. Aaron Hill, who was represented as diving for the prize, expostulated with Pope in a manner so much superior to all mean solicitation, that Pope was reduced to sneak and shuffle, sometimes to deny, and sometimes to apologies; he first endeavours to wound, and is then afraid to own that he meant a blow.

The "Dunciad," in the complete edition, is addressed to Dr. Swift. Of the notes, part were written by Dr. Arbuthnot, and an apologetical letter was prefixed, signed by Cleland, but supposed to have been written by Pope.

After this general war upon dulness, he seems to have indulged himself a while in tranquillity, but his subsequent productions prove that he was not idle. He published (1731) a poem on "Taste," in which he very particularly and severely criticises the house, the furniture, the gardens, and the entertainments of Timon, a man of great wealth and little taste. By Timon he was universally supposed, and by the Earl of Burlington, to whom the poem is addressed, was privately said, to mean the Duke of Chandos, a man perhaps too much delighted with pomp and show, but of a temper kind and beneficent, and who had consequently the voice of the public in his favour. A violent outcry was, therefore, raised against the ingratitude and treachery of Pope, who was said to have been indebted to the patronage of Chandos for a present of a thousand pounds, and who gained the opportunity of insulting him by the kindness of his invitation. The receipt of the thousand pounds Pope publicly denied; but from the reproach which the attack on a character so amiable brought upon him, he tried all means of escaping. The name of Cleland was again employed in an apology, by which no man was satisfied, and he was at last reduced to shelter his temerity behind dissimulation, and endeavour to make that disbelieved which he never had confidence openly to deny. He wrote an exculpatory letter to the duke, which was answered with great magnanimity, as by a man who accepted his excuse without believing his professions. He said that to have ridiculed his taste, or his buildings, had been an indifferent action in another man, but that in Pope, after the reciprocal kindness that had been exchanged between them, it had been less easily excused.

Pope, in one of his letters, complaining of the treatment which his poem had found, "owns that such critics can intimidate him, nay almost persuade him, to write no more, which is a compliment this age deserves." The man who threatens the world is always ridiculous, for the world can easily go on without him, and in a short time will cease to miss him. I have heard of an idiot, who used to revenge his vexatious by lying all night upon the bridge. "There is nothing," says Juvenal, "that a man will not believe in his own favour." Pope had been flattered till he thought himself one of the moving powers in the system of life. When he talked of laying down his pen, those who sat round him entreated and implored; and self-love did not suffer him to suspect that they went away and laughed.

The following year deprived him of Gay, a man whom he had known early, and whom he seemed to love with more tenderness than any other of his literary friends. Pope was now forty-four years old, an age at which the mind begins less easily to admit new confidence, and the will to grow less flexible, and when, therefore, the departure of an old friend is very acutely felt. In the next year (1733) he lost his mother, not by an unexpected death, for she had lasted to the age of ninety-three. But she did not die unlamented. The filial piety of Pope was in the highest degree amiable and exemplary. His parents had the happiness of living till he was at the summit of poetical reputation, till he was at ease in his fortune, and without a rival in his fame, and found no diminution of his respect or tenderness. Whatever was his pride, to them he was obedient; and whatever was his irritability, to them he was gentle. Life has, among its soothing and quiet comforts, few things better to give than such a son.

One of the passages of Pope's life, which seems to deserve some inquiry, was a publication of "Letters" between him and many of his friends, which, falling into the hands of Curll, a rapacious bookseller, of no good fame, were by him printed and sold. This volume containing some letters from noblemen, Pope incited a prosecution against him in the House of Lords for breach of privilege, and attended himself to stimulate the resentment of his friends. Curll appeared at the bar, and, knowing himself in no great danger, spoke of Pope with very little reverence. "He has," said Curll, "a knack at versifying, but in prose I think myself a match for him." When the orders of the House were examined, none of them appeared to have been infringed. Curll went away triumphant, and Pope was left to seek some other remedy.

Curll's account was, that one evening a man in a clergyman's gown, but with a lawyer's band, brought and offered for sale a number of printed volumes, which he found to be Pope's epistolary correspondence; that he asked no name, and was told none, but gave the price demanded, and thought himself authorised to use his purchase to his own advantage. That Curll gave a true account of the transaction it is reasonable to believe, because no falsehood was ever detected; and when, some years afterwards, I mentioned it to Lintot, the son of Bernard, he declared his opinion to be, that Pope knew better than anybody else how Curll obtained the copies, because another parcel was at the same time sent to himself, for which no price had ever been demanded, as he made known his resolution not to pay a porter, and consequently not to deal with a nameless agent. Such care had been taken to make them public, that they were sent at once to two booksellers; to Curll, who was likely to seize them as a prey, and to Lintot, who might he expected to give Pope information of the seeming injury. Lintot, I believe, did nothing, and Curll did what was expected. That to make them public was the only purpose may be reasonably supposed, because the numbers offered to sale by the private messengers showed that the hope of gain could not have been the motive of the impression. It seems that Pope, being desirous of printing his "Letters," and not knowing how to do, without imputation of vanity, what has in this country been done very rarely, contrived an appearance of compulsion, that, when he could complain that his "Letters" were surreptitiously published, he might decently and defensively publish them himself.

Pope's private correspondence, thus promulgated, filled the nation with the praises of his candour, tenderness, and benevolence, the purity of his purposes, and the fidelity of his friendship. There were some letters which a very good or a wise man would wish suppressed; but, as they had been already exposed, it was impracticable now to retract them. From the perusal of those letters, Mr. Allen first conceived the desire of knowing him; and with so much zeal did he cultivate the friendship which he had newly formed, that, when Pope told his purpose of vindicating his own property by a genuine edition, he offered to pay the cost. This, however, Pope did not accept; but in time solicited a subscription for a quarto volume, which appeared (1737), I believe, with sufficient profit. In the preface he tells that his letters were reposited in a friend's library, said to be the Earl of Oxford's, and that the copy thence stolen was sent to the press. The story was doubtless received with different degrees of credit. It may be suspected that the preface to the "Miscellanies" was written to prepare the public for such an incident; and, to strengthen this opinion, James Worsdale, a painter, who was employed in clandestine negotiations, but whose voracity was very doubtful, declared that he was the messenger who carried, by Pope's direction, the books to Curll. When they were thus published and avowed, as they had relation to recent facts, and persons either then living or not yet forgotten, they may be supposed to have found readers; but, as the facts were minute, and the characters being either private or literary, were little known, or little regarded, they awaked no popular kindness or resentment. The book never became much the subject of conversation. Some read it as a contemporary history, and some perhaps as a model of epistolary language; but those who read it did not talk of it. Not much therefore was added by it to fame or envy, nor do I remember that it produced either public praise or public censure. It had, however, in some degree, the recommendation of novelty. Our language had few letters, except those of statesmen. Howel, indeed, about a century ago, published his "Letters," which are commended by Morhoff, and which alone, of his hundred volumes, continue his memory. Loveday's "Letters" were printed only once; those of Herbert and Suckling are hardly known. Mrs. Phillips's (Orinda's) are equally neglected. And those of Walsh seem written as exercises, and were never sent to any living mistress or friend. Pope's epistolary excellence had an open field; he had no English rival, living or dead.

Pope is seen in this collection as connected with the other contemporary wits, and certainly suffers no disgrace in the comparison; but it must be remembered that he had the power of favouring himself. He might have originally had publication in his mind, and have written with care, or have afterwards selected those which he had most happily conceived or most diligently laboured; and I know not whether there does not appear something more studied and artificial in his productions than the rest, except one long letter by Bolingbroke, composed with all the skill and industry of a professed author. It is indeed not easy to distinguish affectation from habit; he that has once studiously formed a style, rarely writes afterwards with complete ease. Pope may be said to write always with his reputation in his head; Swift, perhaps, like a man that remembered he was writing to Pope; but Arbuthnot, like one who lets thoughts drop from his pen as they rise into his mind. Before these "Letters" appeared he published the first part of what he persuaded himself to think a system of Ethics, under the title of an "Essay on Man," which, if his letter to Swift (of September 14, 1723), be rightly explained by the commentator, had been eight years under his consideration, and of which he seems to have desired the success with great solicitude. He had now many open, and doubtless many secret, enemies. The "Dunces" were yet smarting from the war, and the superiority which he publicly arrogated disposed the world to wish his humiliation. All this he knew, and against all this he provided. His own name, and that of his friend to whom the work is inscribed, were in the first editions carefully suppressed; and the poem being of a new kind was ascribed to one or another as favour determined or conjecture wandered. It was given, says Warburton, to every man except him only who could write it. Those who like only when they like the author, and who are under the dominion of a name, condemned it, and those admired it who are willing to scatter praise at random, which, while it is unappropriated, excites no envy. Those friends of Pope that were trusted with the secret went about lavishing honours on the new-born poet, and hinting that Pope was never so much in danger from any former rival. To those authors whom he had personally offended, and to those whose opinion the world considered as decisive, and whom he suspected of envy or malevolence, he sent his Essay as a present before publication, that they might defeat their own enemity by praises which they could not afterwards decently retract. With these precautions, in 1733, was published the first part of the "Essay on Man." There had been for some time a report that Pope was busy upon a "System of Morality," but this design was not discovered in the new poem, which had a form and a title with which its readers were unacquainted. Its reception was not uniform. Some thought it a very imperfect piece, though not without good lines. While the author was unknown, some, as will always happen, favoured him as an adventurer, and some censured him as an intruder, but all thought him above neglect. The sale increased, and editions were multiplied. The subsequent editions of the first epistle exhibited two memorable corrections. At first, the poet and his friend

"Expatiate freely o'er this scene of man, A mighty maze OF WALKS WITHOUT A PLAN;"

for which he wrote afterwards,

"A mighty maze, BUT NOT WITHOUT A PLAN;"

for if there was no plan it was in vain to describe or to trace the maze.

The other alteration was of these lines:-

"And spike of pride, AND IN THY REASON'S SPITE, One truths is clear, whatever is, is right:

but having afterwards discovered, or been shown, that the "truth" which subsisted "in spite of reason" could not be very "clear," he substituted

"And spite of pride IN ERRING REASON'S SPITE."

To such oversights will the most vigorous mind be liable when it is employed at once upon argument and poetry.

The second and third epistles were published, and Pope was, I believe, more and more suspected of writing them. At last, in 1734, he avowed the fourth, and claimed the honour of a moral poet. In the conclusion it is sufficiently acknowledged that the doctrine of the "Essay on Man" was received from Bolingbroke, who is said to have ridiculed Pope, among those who enjoyed his confidence, as having adopted and advanced principles of which he did not perceive the consequence, and as blindly propagating opinions contrary to his own. That those communications had been consolidated into a scheme regularly drawn, and delivered to Pope, from whom it returned only transformed from prose to verse, has been reported, but hardly can be true. The essay plainly appears the fabric of a poet; what Bolingbroke supplied could be only the first principles, the order, illustration, and embellishments, must all be Pope's. These principles it is not my business to clear from obscurity, dogmatism, or falsehood, but they were not immediately examined. Philosophy and poetry have not often the same readers; and the essay abounded in splendid amplifications and sparkling sentences, which were read and admired with no great attention to their ultimate purpose. Its flowers caught the eye, which did not see what the gay foliage concealed, and for a time flourished in the sunshine of universal approbation. So little was any evil tendency discovered, that, as innocence is unsuspicious, many read it for a manual of piety. Its reputation soon invited a translator. It was first turned into French prose, and afterwards by Resnel into verse. Both translations fell into the hands of Crousaz, who first, when he had the version in prose, wrote a general censure, and afterwards reprinted Resnel's version, with particular remarks upon every paragraph.

Crousaz was a professor of Switzerland, eminent for his treatise of logic, and his "Examen de Pyrrhonisme," and, however little known or regarded here, was no mean antagonist. His mind was one of those in which philosophy and piety are happily united. He was accustomed to argument and disquisition, and perhaps was grown too desirous of detecting faults, but his intentions were always right, his opinions were solid, and his religion pure. His incessant vigilance for the promotion of piety disposed him to look with distrust upon all metaphysical systems of theology, and all schemes of virtue and happiness purely rational; and therefore it was not long before he was persuaded that the positions of Pope, as they terminated for the most part in natural religion, were intended to draw mankind away from revelation, and to represent the whole course of things as a necessary concatenation of indissoluble fatality, and it is undeniable that in many passages a religious eye may easily discover expressions not very favourable to morals or to liberty.

About this time Warburton began to make his appearance in the first ranks of learning. He was a man of vigorous faculties, a mind fervid and vehement, supplied by incessant and unlimited inquiry, with wonderful extent and variety of knowledge, which yet had not oppressed his imagination nor clouded his perspicacity. To every work he brought a memory full fraught, together with a fancy fertile of original combinations and at once exerted the powers of the scholar, the reasoner, and the wit. But his knowledge was too multifarious to be always exact, and his pursuits were too eager to be always cautions. His abilities gave him a haughty confidence, which he disdained to conceal or mollify, and his impatience of opposition disposed him to treat his adversaries with such contemptuous superiority as made his readers commonly his enemies, and excited against the advocate the wishes of some who favoured the cause. He seems to have adopted the Roman Emperor's determination, oderint dum metuant; he used no allurements of gentle language, but wished to compel rather than persuade. His style is copious without selection, and forcible without neatness. He took the words that presented themselves. His diction is coarse and impure, and his sentences are unmeasured. He had in the early part of his life pleased himself with the notice of inferior wits, and corresponded with the enemies of Pope. A letter was produced, when he had perhaps himself forgotten it, in which he tells Concanen, "Dryden, I observe, borrows for want of leisure, and Pope for want of genius, Milton out of pride, and Addison out of modesty." And when Theobald published Shakespeare, in opposition to Pope, the best notes were supplied by Warburton. But the time was now come when Warburton was to change his opinion, and Pope was to find a defender in him who had contributed so much to the exaltation of his rival.

The arrogance of Warburton excited against him every artifice of offence, and therefore it may be supposed that his union with Pope was censured as hypocritical inconstancy, but surely to think differently at different times of poetical merit may be easily allowed. Such opinions are often admitted, and dismissed without nice examination. Who is there that has not found reason for changing his mind about questions of greater importance?

Warburton, whatever was his motive, undertook, without solicitation, to rescue Pope from the talons of Crousaz, by freeing him from the imputation of favouring fatality or rejecting revelation; and from month to month continued a vindication of the "Essay on Man," in the literary journal of that time called the "Republic of Letters."

Pope, who probably began to doubt the tendency of his own work, was glad that the positions, of which he perceived himself not to know the full meaning, could by any mode of interpretation be made to mean well. How much he was pleased with his gratuitous defender the following letter evidently shows:-

"April 11, 1739.

"Sir,--I have just received from Mr. R. two more of your letters. It is in the greatest hurry imaginable that I write this; but I cannot help thanking you in particular for your third letter, which is so extremely clear, short, and full, that I think Mr. Crousaz ought never to have another answer, and deserved not so good an one. I can only say, you do him too much honour, and me too much right, so odd as the expression seems; for you have made my system as clear as I ought to have done, and could not. It is indeed the same system as mine, but illustrated with a ray of your own, as they say our natural body is the same still when it is glorified. I am sure I like it better than I did before, and so will every man else. I know I meant just what you explain; but I did not explain my own meaning so well as you. You understand me as well as I do myself; but you express me better than I could express myself. Pray accept the sincerest acknowledgments. I cannot but wish these letters were put together in one book, and intend (with your leave) to procure a translation of part at least, or of all of them, into French; but I shall not proceed a step without your consent and opinion," &c.

By this fond and eager acceptance of an exculpatory comment Pope testified that, whatever might be the seeming or real import of the principles which he had received from Bolingbroke, he had not intentionally attacked religion; and Bolingbroke, if he meant to make him, without his own consent, an instrument of mischief, found him now engaged, with his eyes open, on the side of truth. It is known that Bolingbroke concealed from Pope his real opinions. He once discovered them to Mr. Hooke, who related them again to Pope, and was told by him that he must have mistaken the meaning of what he heard: and Bolingbroke, when Pope's uneasiness incited him to desire an explanation, declared that Hooke had misunderstood him.

Bolingbroke hated Warburton, who had drawn his pupil from him; and a little before Pope's death they had a dispute, from which they parted with mutual aversion. From this time Pope lived in the closest intimacy with his commentator, and amply rewarded his kindness and his zeal, for he introduced him to Mr. Murray, by whose interest he became preacher at Lincoln's Inn, and to Mr. Allen, who gave him his niece and his estate, and by consequence a bishopric. When he died, he left him the property of his works, a legacy which may be reasonably estimated at four thousand pounds.

Pope's fondness for the "Essay on Man" appeared by his desire of its propagation. Dobson, who had gained reputation by his version of Prior's "Solomon," was employed by him to translate it into Latin verse, and was for that purpose some time at Twickenham; but he left his work, whatever was the reason, unfinished; and, by Benson's invitation, undertook the longer task of "Paradise Lost." Pope then desired his friend to find a scholar who should turn his essay into Latin prose; but no such performance has ever appeared.

Pope lived at this time AMONG THE GREAT, with that reception and respect to which his works entitled him, and which he had not impaired by any private misconduct or factious partiality. Though Bolingbroke was his friend, Walpole was not his enemy, but treated him with so much consideration as, at his request, to solicit and obtain from the French Minister an abbey for Mr. Southcot, whom he considered himself as obliged to reward, by his exertion of his interest, for the benefit which he had received from his attendance in a long illness. It was said, that when the Court was at Richmond, Queen Caroline had declared her intention to visit him. This may have been only a careless effusion, thought on no more. The report of such notice, however, was soon in many mouths; and, if I do not forget or misapprehend Savage's account, Pope, pretending to decline what was not yet offered, left his house for a time, not, I suppose, for any other reason than lest he should be thought to stay at home in expectation of an honour which would not be conferred. He was therefore angry at Swift, who represents him as "refusing the visits of a queen," because he knew that what had never been offered had never been refused.

Beside the general system of morality, supposed to be contained in the "Essay on Man," it was his intention to write distinct poems upon the different duties or conditions of life, one of which is the "Epistle to Lord Bathurst" (1733) on the "Use of Riches," a piece on which he declared great labour to have been bestowed. Into this poem some hints are historically thrown, and some known characters are introduced, with others of which it is difficult to say how far they are real or fictitious: but the praise of Kryle, the Man of Ross, deserves particular examination, who, after a long and pompous enumeration of his public works and private charities, is said to have diffused all those blessings from five hundred a year. Wonders are willingly told and willingly heard. The truth is, that Kyrle was a man of known integrity and active benevolence, by whose solicitation the wealthy were persuaded to pay contributions to his charitable schemes. This influence he obtained by an example of liberality exerted to the utmost extent of his power, and was thus enabled to give more than he had. This account Mr. Victor received from the minister of the place, and I have preserved it, that the praise of a good man, being made more credible, may be more solid. Narrations of romantic and impracticable virtue will be read with wonder, but that which is unattainable is recommended in vain; that good may be endeavoured it must be shown to be possible. This is the only piece in which the author has given a hint of his religion, by ridiculing the ceremony of burning the Pope, and by mentioning with some indignation the inscription on the Monument.

When this poem was first published, the dialogue having no letters of direction was perplexed and obscure. Pope seems to have written with no very distinct idea, for he calls that an "Epistle to Bathurst," in which Bathurst is introduced as speaking. He afterwards (1734) inscribed to Lord Cobham his "Characters of Men," written with close attention to the operations of the mind and modifications of life. In this poem he has endeavoured to establish and exemplify his favourite theory of the RULING PASSION, by which he means an original direction of desire to some particular object, an innate affection which gives all action a determinate and invariable tendency, and operates upon the whole system of life, either openly, cut more secretly by the intervention of some accidental or subordinate propension. Of any passion, thus innate and irresistible, the existence may reasonably be doubted. Human characters are by no means constant; men change by change of place, of fortune, of acquaintance. He who is at one time a lover of pleasure, is at another a lover of money. Those, indeed, who attain any excellence commonly spend life in one pursuit, for excellence is not often gained upon easier terms. But to the particular species of excellence men are directed, not by an ascendant planet or predominating humour, but by the first book which they read, some early conversation which they heard, or some accident which excited ardour and emulation. It must at least be allowed that this ruling passion, antecedent to reason and observation, must have an object independent on human contrivance, for there can be no natural desire of artificial good. No man, therefore, can be born, in the strict acceptation, a lover of money, for he may be born where money does not exist; nor can he be born in a moral sense a lover of his country, for society politically regulated is a state contradistinguished from a state of nature, and any attention to that coalition of interests which makes the happiness of a country is possible only to those whom inquiry and reflection have enabled to comprehend it. This doctrine is in itself pernicious as well as false; its tendency is to produce the belief of a kind of moral predestination or over-ruling principle which cannot be resisted. He that admits it is prepared to comply with every desire that caprice or opportunity shall excite, and to flatter himself that he submits only to the lawful dominion of nature in obeying the resistless authority of his ruling passion.

Pope has formed his theory with so little skill that in the examples by which he illustrates and confirms it he has confounded passions, appetites, and habits. To the "Characters of Men" he added soon after, in an epistle supposed to have been addressed to Martha Blount, but which the last edition has taken from her, the "Characters of Women." This poem, which was laboured with great diligence and in the author's opinion with great success, was neglected at its first publication, as the commentator supposes, because the public was informed by an advertisement that it contained no character drawn from the life, an assertion which Pope probably did not expect nor wished to have been believed, and which he soon gave his readers sufficient reason to distrust, by telling them in a note that the work was imperfect because part of his subject was vice too high to be yet exposed. The time, however, soon came in which it was safe to display the Duchess of Marlborough under the name of Atossa, and her character was inserted with no great honour to the writer's gratitude.

He published from time to time (between 1730 and 1740) imitations of different poems of Horace, generally with his name, and once, as was suspected, without it. What he was upon moral principles ashamed to own he ought to have suppressed. Of these pieces it is useless to settle the dates, as they had seldom much relation to the times, and perhaps had been long in his hands. This mode of imitation, in which the ancients are familiarised by adapting their sentiments to modern topics, by making Horace say of Shakespeare what he originally said of Ennius, and accommodating his satires on Pantolabus and Nomentanus to the flatterers and prodigals of our own time, was first practised in the reign of Charles the Second, by Oldham and Rochester, at least I remember no instances more ancient. It is a kind of middle composition between translation and original design, which pleases when the thoughts are unexpectedly applicable, and the parallels lucky. It seems to have been Pope's favourite amusement, for he has carried it farther than any former poet. He published likewise a revival, in smoother numbers, of Dr. Donne's "Satires," which was recommended to him by the Duke of Shrewsbury and the Earl of Oxford. They made no great impression on the public. Pope seems to have known their imbecility and therefore suppressed them while he was yet contending to rise in reputation, but ventured them when he thought their deficiencies more likely to be imputed to Donne than to himself.

The "Epistle to Dr. Arbuthnot," which seems to be derived in its first design from Boileau's Address a son Esprit, was published in January, 1735, about a month before the death of him to whom it is inscribed. It is to be regretted that either honour or pleasure should have been missed by Arbuthnot, a man estimable for his learning, amiable for his life, and venerable for his piety. Arbuthnot was a man of great comprehension, skilful in his profession, versed in the sciences, acquainted with ancient literature, and able to animate his mass of knowledge by a bright and active imagination; a scholar with great brilliance of wit, a wit who, in the crowd of life, retained and discovered a noble ardour of religious zeal. In this poem Pope seems to reckon with the public. He vindicates himself from censures, and with dignity rather than arrogance enforces his own claims to kindness and respect. Into this poem are interwoven several paragraphs which had been before printed, as a fragment, and among them the satirical lines upon Addison, of which the last couplet has been twice corrected. It was at first -

"Who would not smile if such a man there be? Who would not laugh if Addison were he?"

Then -

"Who would not grieve if such a man there be? Who would not laugh if Addison were he?"

At last it is -

"Who but must laugh if such a man there he? Who would not weep if Atticus were he?"

He was at this time at open war with Lord Hervey, who had distinguished himself as a steady adherent to the ministry, and being offended with a contemptuous answer to one of his pamphlets, had summoned Pulteney to a duel. Whether he or Pope made the first attack perhaps cannot now be easily known. He had written an invective against Pope, whom he calls, "Hard as thy heart, and as thy birth obscure;" and hints that his father was a hatter. To this Pope wrote a reply in verse and prose. The verses are in this poem, and the prose, though it was never sent, is printed among his letters; but to a cool reader of the present time exhibits nothing but tedious malignity.

His last "Satires" of the general kind, were two Dialogues, named, from the year in which they were published, "Seventeen hundred and thirty-eight." In these poems many are praised and many reproached. Pope was then entangled in the opposition, a follower of the Prince of Wales, who dined at his house, and the friend of many who obstructed and censured the conduct of the ministers. His political partiality was too plainly shown; he forgot the prudence with which he passed, in his earlier years, uninjured and unoffending, through much more violent conflicts of faction. In the first Dialogue, having an opportunity of praising Allen of Bath, he asked his leave to mention him as a man not illustrious by any merit of his ancestors, and called him in his verses "low-born Allen." Men are seldom satisfied with praise introduced or followed by any mention of defect. Allen seems not to have taken any pleasure in his epithet, which was afterwards softened into "humble Allen." In the second Dialogue he took some liberty with one of the Foxes among others; which Fox in a reply to Lyttelton, took an opportunity of repaying, by reproaching him with the friendship of a lampooner, who scattered his ink without fear or decency, and against whom he hoped the resentment of the Legislature would quickly be discharged.

About this time Paul Whitehead, a small poet, was summoned before the Lords for a poem called "Manners," together with Dodsley, his publisher. Whitehead, who hung loose upon society, skulked and escaped, but Dodsley's shop and family made his appearance necessary. He was, however, soon dismissed, and the whole process was probably intended rather to intimidate Pope than to punish Whitehead.

Pope never afterwards attempted to join the patriot with the poet, nor drew his pen upon statesmen. That he desisted from his attempts of reformation is imputed by his commentator to his despair of prevailing over the corruption of the time. He was not likely to have been ever of opinion that the dread of his satire would countervail the love of power or of money; he pleased himself with being important and formidable, and gratified sometimes his pride, and sometimes his resentment, till at last he began to think he should be more safe if he were less busy.

The "Memoirs of Scriblerus," published about this time, extend only to the first book of a work projected in concert by Pope, Swift, and Arbuthnot, who used to meet on the time of Queen Anne, and denominated themselves the "Scriblerus Club." Their purpose was to censure the abuses of learning by a fictitious life of an infatuated scholar. They were dispersed; the design was never completed, and Warburton laments its miscarriage as an event very disastrous to polite letters. If the whole may be estimated by this specimen, which seems to be the production of Arbuthnot, with a few touches perhaps by Pope, the want of more will not be much lamented; for the follies which the writer ridicules are so little practised that they are not known; nor can the satire be understood but by the learned. He raises phantoms of absurdity, and then drives them away. He cures diseases that were never felt. For this reason this joint production of three great writers has never obtained any notice from mankind. It has been little read, or when read has been forgotten, as no man could be wiser, better, or merrier, by remembering it. The design cannot boast of much originality; for, besides its general resemblance to "Don Quixote," there will be found in it particular imitations of the "History of Mr. Ouffle."

Swift carried so much of it into Ireland as supplied him with hints for his "Travels;" and with those the world might have been contented, though the rest had been suppressed.

Pope had sought for images and sentiments in a region not known to have been explored by many other of the English writers. He had consulted the modern writers of Latin poetry, a class of authors whom Boileau endeavoured to bring into contempt, and who are too generally neglected. Pope, however, was not ashamed of their acquaintance, nor ungrateful for the advantages which he might have derived from it. A small selection from the Italians, who wrote in Latin, had been published at London, about the latter end of the last century, by a man who concealed his name, but whom his preface shows to have been qualified for his undertaking. This collection Pope amplified by more than half, and (1740) published it in two volumes, but injuriously omitted his predecessor's preface. To these books, which had nothing but the mere text, no regard was paid; the authors were still neglected, and the editor was neither praised nor censured. He did not sink into idleness; he had planned a work, which he considered as subsequent to his "Essay on Man," of which he has given this account to Dr. Swift:-

"March 25, 1736.

"If ever I write any more Epistles in verse, one of them shall be addressed to you. I have long concerted it and begun it; but I would make what bears your name as finished as my last work ought to be, that is to say, more finished than any of the rest. The subject is large, and will divide into four Epistles, which naturally follow the 'Essay on Man,' viz: 1. Of the Extent and Limits of Human Reason and Science. 2. A view of the useful and therefore attainable, and of the unuseful and therefore unattainable Arts. 3. Of the Nature, Ends, Application, and Use, of different Capacities. 4. Of the Use of Learning, of the Science, of the World, and of Wit. It will conclude with a satire against the misapplication of all these, exemplified by Pictures, Characters, and Examples."

This work in its full extent--being now afflicted with an asthma, and finding the powers of life gradually declining--he had no longer courage to undertake; but, from the materials which he had provided, he added, at Warburton's request, another book to the "Dunciad," of which the design is to ridicule such studies as are either hopeless or useless, as either pursue what is unattainable, or what, if it be attained, is of no use. When this book was printed (1742) the laurel had been for some time upon the head of Cibber, a man whom it cannot be supposed that Pope could regard with much kindness or esteem, though in one of the imitations of Horace he has liberally enough praised the "Careless Husband." In the "Dunciad," among other worthless scribblers, he had mentioned Cibber, who, in his "Apology," complains of the great Poet's unkindness as more injurious, "because," says he, "I never have offended him."

It might have been expected that Pope should have been in some degree mollified by this submissive gentleness, but no such consequence appeared. Though he condescended to commend Cibber once, he mentioned him afterwards contemptuously in one of his satires, and again in his "Epistle to Arbuthnot," and in the fourth book of the "Dunciad" attacked him with acrimony, to which the provocation is not easily discoverable. Perhaps he imagined that, in ridiculing the Laureate, he satirised those by whom the laurel had been given, and gratified that ambitious petulance with which he affected to insult the great. The severity of this satire left Cibber no longer any patience. He had confidence enough in his own powers to believe that he could disturb the quiet of his adversary, and doubtless did not want instigators, who, without any care about the victory, desired to amuse themselves by looking on the contest. He therefore gave the town a pamphlet, in which he declares his resolution from that time never to bear another blow without returning it, and to tire out his adversary by perseverance if he cannot conquer him by strength.

The incessant and unappeasable malignity of Pope he imputes to a very distant cause. After the Three Hours After Marriage had been driven off the stage, by the offence which the mummy and crocodile gave the audience, while the exploded scene was yet fresh in memory, it happened that Cibber played Bayes in the Rehearsal; and, as it had been usual to enliven the part by the mention of any recent theatrical transactions, he said, that he once thought to have introduced his lovers disguised in a mummy and a crocodile. "This," says he, "was received with loud claps, which indicated contempt for the play." Pope, who was behind the scenes, meeting him as he left the stage, attacked him, as he says, with all the virulence of a "wit out of his senses;" to which he replied, "that he would take no other notice of what was said by so particular a man, than to declare, that as often as he played that part he would repeat the same provocation." He shows his opinion to be that Pope was one of the authors of the play which he so zealously defended, and adds an idle story of Pope's behaviour at a tavern.

The pamphlet was written with little power of thought or language, and, if suffered to remain without notice, would have been very soon forgotten. Pope had now been enough acquainted with human life to know, if his passion had not been too powerful for his understanding, that, from a contention like his with Cibber, the world seeks nothing but diversion, which is given at the expense of the higher character. When Cibber lampooned Pope, curiosity was excited. What Pope would say of Cibber nobody inquired, but in hope that Pope's asperity might betray his pain and lessen his dignity. He should therefore have suffered the pamphlet to flutter and die, without confessing that it stung him. The dishonour of being shown as Cibber's antagonist could never be compensated by the victory. Cibber had nothing to lose. When Pope had exhausted all his malignity upon him, he would rise in the esteem both of his friends and his enemies. Silence only could have made him despicable; the blow which did not appear to be felt would have been struck in vain. But Pope's irascibility prevailed, and he resolved to tell the whole English world that he was at war with Cibber; and, to show that he thought him to common adversary, he prepared no common vengeance. He published a new edition of the "Dunciad," in which he degraded Theobald from his painful pre-eminence, and enthroned Cibber in his stead. Unhappily the two heroes were of opposite characters, and Pope was unwilling to lose what he had already written. He has therefore depraved his poem by giving to Cibber the old books, the old pedantry, and the sluggish pertinacity of Theobald.

Pope was ignorant enough of his own interest to make another change, and introduced Osborne contending for a prize among the booksellers. Osborne was a man entirely destitute of shame, without sense of any disgrace but that of poverty. He told me, when he was doing that which raised Pope's resentment, that he should be put into the "Dunciad;" but he had the fate of Cassandra. I gave no credit to his prediction, till in time I saw it accomplished. The shafts of satire were directed equally in vain against Cibber and Osborne; being repelled by the impenetrable impudence of one, and deadened by the impassive dulness of the other. Pope confessed his own pain by his anger; but he gave no pain to those who had provoked him. He was able to hurt none but himself; by transferring the same ridicule from one to another, he reduced himself to the insignificance of his own magpie, who from his cage calls cuckold at a venture.

Cibber, according to his engagement, repaid the "Dunciad" with another pamphlet, which, Pope said, "would be as good as a dose of hartshorn to him;" but his tongue and his heart were at variance. I have heard Mr. Richardson relate that he attended his father the painter on a visit, when one of Cibber's pamphlets came into the hands of Pope, who said, "These things are my diversion." They sat by him while he perused it, and saw his features writhing with anguish: and young Richardson said to his father, when they returned, that he hoped to be preserved from such diversion as had been that day the lot of Pope. From this time, finding his diseases more oppressive, and his vital powers gradually declining, he no longer strained his faculties with any original composition, nor proposed any other employment for his remaining life than the revisal and correction of his former works, in which he received advice and assistance from Warburton, whom he appears to have trusted and honoured in the highest degree. He laid aside his Epic Poem, perhaps without much loss to mankind; for his hero was Brutus the Trojan, who, according to a ridiculous fiction, established a colony in Britain. The subject, therefore, was of the fabulous age; the actors were a race upon whom imagination has been exhausted, and attention wearied, and to whom the mind will not easily be recalled, when it is invited in blank verse, which Pope had adopted with great imprudence, and, I think, without due consideration of the nature of our language. The sketch is, at least in part, preserved by Ruffhead, by which it appears that Pope was thoughtless enough to model the names of his heroes with terminations not consistent with the time or country in which he places them. He lingered through the next year, but perceived himself, as he expresses it, "going down the hill." He had for at least five years been afflicted with an asthma, and other disorders, which his physicians were unable to relieve. Towards the end of his life he consulted Dr. Thomson, a man who had, by large promises, and free censures of the common practice of physic, forced himself up into sudden reputation. Thomson declared his distemper to be a dropsy, and evacuated part of the water by tincture of jalap, but confessed that his belly did not subside. Thomson had many enemies, and Pope was persuaded to dismiss him.

While he was yet capable of amusement and conversation, as he was one day sitting in the air with Lord Bolingbroke and Lord Marchmont, he saw his favourite Martha Blount at the bottom of the terrace, and asked Lord Bolingbroke to go and hand her up. Bolingbroke, not liking his errand, crossed his legs and sat still; but Lord Marchmont, who was younger and less captious, waited on the lady, who, when he came to her, asked, "What, is he not dead yet?" She is said to have neglected him with shameful unkindness, in the latter time of his decay; yet, of the little which he had to leave she had a very great part. Their acquaintance began early; the life of each was pictured on the other's mind; their conversation therefore was endearing, for when they met, there was an immediate coalition of congenial notions. Perhaps he considered her unwillingness to approach the chamber of sickness as female weakness, or human frailty; perhaps he was conscious to himself of peevishness and impatience, or, though he was offended by her inattention, might yet consider her merit as overbalancing her fault; and if he had suffered his heart to be alienated from her, he could have found nothing that might fill her place; he could have only shrunk within himself. It was too late to transfer his confidence or fondness.

In May, 1744, his death was approaching. On the 6th he was all day delirious, which he mentioned for days afterwards as a sufficient humiliation of the vanity of man; he afterwards complained of seeing things as through a curtain, and in false colours, and one day, its the presence of Dodsley, asked what arm it was that came from the wall. He said that his greatest inconvenience was inability to think. Bolingbroke sometimes wept over him in this state of helpless decay; and being told by Spence, that Pope, at the intermission of his deliriousness, was always saying something kind either of his present or absent friends, and that his humanity seemed to have survived his understanding, answered, "It has so." And added, "I never in my life knew a man that had so tender a heart for his particular friends, or more general friendship for mankind." At another time he said, "I have known Pope these thirty years, and value myself more in his friendship than--" His grief then suppressed his voice.

Pope expressed undoubting confidence of a future state. Being asked by his friend Mr. Hooke, a papist, whether he would not die like his father and mother, and whether a priest should not be called, he answered, "I do not think it essential, but it will be very right; and I thank you for putting me in mind of it." In the morning, after the priest had given him the last sacraments, he said "There is nothing that is meritorious but virtue and friendship; and indeed friendship itself is only a part of virtue." He died in the evening of the 30th day of May 1744, so placidly, that the attendants did not discern the exact time of his expiration. He was buried at Twickenham, near his father and mother, where a monument has been erected to him by his commentator, the Bishop of Gloucester.

He left the care of his papers to his executors; first to Lord Bolingbroke, and, if he should not be living, to the Earl of Marchmont, undoubtedly expecting them to be proud of the trust, and eager to extend his fame. But let no man dream of influence beyond his life. After a decent time Dodsley, the bookseller, went to solicit preference as the publisher, and was told that the parcel had not been yet inspected; and, whatever was the reason, the world has been disappointed of what was "reserved for the next age." He lost, indeed, the favour of Bolingbroke by a kind of posthumous offence. The political pamphlet called "The Patriot King" had been put into his hands that he might procure the impression of a very few copies, to be distributed, according to the author's direction, among his friends, and Pope assured him that no more had been printed than were allowed; but, soon after his death, the printer brought and resigned a complete edition of fifteen hundred copies, which Pope had ordered him to print and retain in secret. He kept, as was observed, his engagement to Pope better than Pope had kept it to his friend; and nothing was known of the transaction till, upon the death of his employer, he thought himself obliged to deliver the books to the right owner, who, with great indignation, made a fire in his yard, and delivered the whole impression to the flames.

Hitherto nothing had been done which was not naturally dictated by resentment of violated faith; resentment more acrimonious, as the violator had been more loved or more trusted. But here the anger might have stopped; the injury was private, and there was little danger from the example. Bolingbroke, however, was not yet satisfied. His thirst of vengeance excited him to blast the memory of the man over whom he had wept in his last struggles; and he employed Mallet, another friend of Pope, to tell the tale to the public, with all its aggravations. Warburton, whose heart was warm with his legacy and tender by the recent separation, thought it proper for him to interpose, and undertook, not indeed to vindicate the action, for breach of trust has always something criminal, but to extenuate it by an apology. Having advanced what cannot be denied, that moral obliquity is made more or less excusable by the motives that produce it, he inquires what evil purpose could have induced Pope to break his promise. He could not delight his vanity by usurping the work, which, though not sold in shops, had been shown to a number more than sufficient to preserve the author's claim; he could not gratify his avarice, for he could not sell his plunder till Bolingbroke was dead; and even then, if the copy was left to another, his fraud would be defeated, and if left to himself would be useless.

Warburton therefore supposes, with great appearance of reason, that the irregularity of his conduct proceeded wholly from his zeal for Bolingbroke, who might perhaps have destroyed the pamphlet, which Pope thought it his duty to preserve, even without its author's approbation. To this apology an answer was written in "A letter to the most impudent man living." He brought some reproach upon his own memory by the petulant and contemptuous mention made in his will of Mr. Allen and an affected repayment of his benefactions. Mrs. Blount, as the known friend and favourite of Pope, had been invited to the house of Allen, where she comported herself with such indecent arrogance that she parted from Mrs. Allen in a state of irreconcilable dislike, and the door was for ever barred against her. This exclusion she resented with so much bitterness as to refuse any legacy from Pope unless he left the world with a disavowal of obligation to Allen. Having been long under her dominion, now tottering in the decline of life, and unable to resist the violence of her temper, or perhaps, with the prejudice of a lover, persuaded that she had suffered improper treatment, he complied with her demand, and polluted his will with female resentment. Allen accepted the legacy, which he gave to the hospital at Bath, observing that Pope was always a bad accountant, and that if to 150 pounds he had put a cipher more he had come nearer to the truth.

The person of Pope is well known not to have been formed by the nicest model. He has, in his account of the "Little Club," compared himself to a spider, and by another is described as protuberant behind and before. He is said to have been beautiful in his infancy, but he was of a constitution originally feeble and weak; and, as bodies of a tender frame are easily distorted, his deformity was probably in part the effect of his application. His stature was so low, that to bring him to a level with common tables, it was necessary to raise his seat. But his face was not displeasing, and his eyes were animated and vivid. By natural deformity, or accidental distortion, his vital functions were so much disordered, that his life was "a long disease." His most frequent assailant was the headache, which he used to relieve by inhaling the steam of coffee, which he very frequently required.

Most of what can be told concerning his petty peculiarities was communicated by a female domestic of the Earl of Oxford, who knew him perhaps after the middle of life. He was then so weak as to stand in perpetual need of female attendance; extremely sensible of cold, so that he wore a kind of fur doublet, under a shirt of a very coarse warm linen with fine sleeves. When he rose, he was invested in bodice made of stiff canvas, being scarcely able to hold himself erect till they were laced, and he then put on a flannel waistcoat. One side was contracted. His legs were so slender, that he enlarged their bulk with three pairs of stockings, which were drawn on and off by the maid, for he was not able to dress or undress himself, and neither went to bed nor rose without help. His weakness made it very difficult for him to be clean. His hair had fallen almost all away, and he used to dine sometimes with Lord Oxford, privately, in a velvet cap. His dress of ceremony was black, with a tie-wig, and a little sword. The indulgence and accommodation which his sickness required, had taught him all the unpleasing and unsocial qualities of a valetudinary man. He expected that everything should give way to his ease or humour, as a child, whose parents will not hear her cry, has an unresisted dominion in the nursery.

"C'est que l'enfant toujours est homme, C'est que l'homme est toujours enfant."

When he wanted to sleep he "nodded in company," and once slumbered at his own table while the Prince of Wales was talking of poetry.

The reputation which his friendship gave procured him many invitations, but he was a very troublesome inmate. He brought no servant, and had so many wants, that a numerous attendance was scarcely able to supply them. Wherever he was, he left no room for another, because he exacted the attention, and employed the activity of the whole family. His errands were so frequent and frivolous, that the footmen in time avoided and neglected him, and the Earl of Oxford discharged some of his servants for their resolute refusal of his messages. The maids, when they had neglected their business, alleged that they had been employed by Mr. Pope. One of his constant demands was of coffee in the night, and to the woman that waited on him in his chamber he was very burthensome. But he was careful to recompense her want of sleep, and Lord Oxford's servant declared, that in the house where her business was to answer his call, she would not ask for wages. He had another fault, easily incident to those who, suffering much pain, think themselves entitled to what pleasures they can snatch. He was too indulgent to his appetite: he loved meat highly seasoned and of strong taste; and, at the intervals of the table, amused himself with biscuits and dry conserves. If he sat down to a variety of dishes, he would oppress his stomach with repletion; and though he seemed angry when a dram was offered him, did not forbear to drink it. His friends, who knew the avenues to his heart, pampered him with presents of luxury, which he did not suffer to stand neglected. The death of great men is not always proportioned to the lustre of their lives. Hannibal, says Juvenal, did not perish by the javelin or the sword, the slaughters of Cannae were revenged by a ring. The death of Pope was imputed by some of his friends to a silver saucepan, in which it was his delight to eat potted lampreys. That he loved too well to eat is certain; but that his sensuality shortened his life will not be hastily concluded, when it is remembered that a conformation so irregular lasted six-and-fifty years, notwithstanding such pertinacious diligence of study and meditation. In all his intercourse with mankind he had great delight in artifice, and endeavoured to attain all his purposes by indirect and unsuspected methods. "He hardly drank tea without a stratagem." If at the house of friends he wanted any accommodation, he was not willing to ask for it in plain terms, but would mention it remotely as something convenient; though when it was procured, he soon made it appear for whose sake it had been recommended. Thus he teased Lord Orrery till he obtained a screen. He practised his arts on such small occasions, that Lady Bolingbroke used to say, in a French phrase, that "he played the politician about cabbages and turnips." His unjustifiable impression of the "Patriot King," as it can be attributed to no particular motive, must have proceeded from his general habit of secrecy and cunning; he caught an opportunity of a sly trick, and pleased himself with the thought of outwitting Bolingbroke. In familiar or convivial conversation, it does not appear that he excelled. He may be said to have resembled Dryden, as being not one that was distinguished by vivacity in company. It is remarkable that, so near his time, so much should be known of what he has written, and so little of what he has said: traditional memory retains no sallies of raillery, nor sentences of observation: nothing either pointed or solid, either wise or merry. One apophthegm only stands upon record. When an objection, raised against his inscription for Shakespeare, was defended by the authority of Patrick, he replied, horresco referens, that he "would allow the publisher of a dictionary to know the meaning of a single word, but not of two words put together."

He was fretful and easily displeased, and allowed himself to be capriciously resentful. He would sometimes leave Lord Oxford silently, no one could tell why, and was to be courted back by more letters and messages than the footmen were willing to carry. The table was indeed infested by Lady Mary Wortley, who was the friend of Lady Oxford, and who, knowing his peevishness, could by no entreaties be restrained from contradicting him, till their disputes were sharpened to such asperity, that one or the other quitted the house. He sometimes condescended to be jocular with servants or inferiors; but by no merriment, either of others or his own, was he ever seen excited to laughter.

Of his domestic character, frugality was a part eminently remarkable. Having determined not to be dependent, he determined not to be in want, and therefore wisely and magnanimously rejected all temptations to expense unsuitable to his fortune. This general care must be universally approved; but it sometimes appeared in petty artifices of parsimony, such as the practice of writing his compositions on the back of letters, as may be seen in the remaining copy of the "Iliad," by which perhaps in five years five shillings were saved; or in a niggardly reception of his friends, and scantiness of entertainment, as, when he had two guests in his house, he would set at supper a single pint upon the table; and having himself taken two small glasses, would retire, and say, "Gentlemen. I leave you to your wine." Yet he tells his friends that "he has a heart for all, a house for all, and whatever they may think, a fortune for all." He sometimes, however, made a splendid dinner, and is said to have wanted no part of the skill or elegance which such performances require. That this magnificence should be often displayed, that obstinate prudence with which he conducted his affairs would not permit; for his revenue, certain and casual, amounted only to about eight hundred pounds a year, of which, however, he declares himself able to assign one hundred to charity. Of this fortune, which, as it arose from public approbation, was very honourably obtained, his imagination seems to have been too full: it would be hard to find a man so well entitled to notice by his wit, that ever delighted so much in talking of his money. In his Letters and in his poems, his garden and his grotto, his quincunx and his vines, or some hints of his opulence, are always to be found. The great topic of his ridicule is poverty; the crimes with which he reproaches his antagonists are their debts, their habitation in the Mint, and their want of a dinner. He seems to be of an opinion not very uncommon in the world, that to want money is to want everything. Next to the pleasure of contemplating his possessions, seems to be that of enumerating the men of high rank with whom he was acquainted, and whose notice he loudly proclaims not to have been obtained by any practices of meanness or servility; a boast which was never denied to be true, and to which very few poets have ever aspired. Pope never set genius to sale; he never flattered those whom he did not love, nor praised those whom he did not esteem. Savage, however, remarked that he began a little to relax his dignity when he wrote a distich for "his Highness's dog."

His admiration of the great seems to have increased in the advance of life. He passed over peers and statesmen to inscribe his "Iliad" to Congreve, with a magnanimity of which the praise had been complete, had his friend's virtue been equal to his wit. Why he was chosen for so great an honour, it is not now possible to know; there is no trace in literary history of any particular intimacy between them. The name of Congreve appears in the Letters among those of his other friends, but without any observable distinction or consequence. To his latter works, however, he took care to annex names dignified with titles, but was not very happy in his choice; for, except Lord Bathurst, none of his noble friends were such as that a good man would wish to have his intimacy with them known to posterity; he can derive little honour from the notice of Cobham, Burlington, or Bolingbroke.

Of his social qualities, if an estimate be made from his Letters, an opinion too favourable cannot easily be formed; they exhibit a perpetual and unclouded effulgence of general benevolence, and particular fondness. There is nothing but liberality, gratitude, constancy, and tenderness. It has been so long said as to be commonly believed, that the true characters of men may be found in their letters, and that he who writes to his friend lays his heart open before him. But the truth is that such were the simple friendships of the Golden Age, and are now the friendships only of children. Very few can boast of hearts which they dare lay open to themselves, and of which, by whatever accident exposed, they do not shun a distinct and continued view; and, certainly, who we hide from ourselves we do not show to our friend. There is, indeed, no transaction which offers strange temptations to fallacy and sophistication than epistolary intercourse. In the eagerness of conversation the first emotions of the mind often burst out before they are considered; in the tumult of business, interest and passion have their genuine effect; but a friendly letter is a calm and deliberate performance in the cool of leisure, in the stillness of solitude, and surely no man sits down to depreciate by design his own character.

Friendship has no tendency to secure veracity; for by whom can a man so much wish to be thought better than he is, as by him whose kindness he desires to gain or keep? Even in writing to the world there is less constraint; the author is not confronted with his reader, and takes his chance of approbation among the different dispositions of mankind; but a letter is addressed to a single mind, of which the prejudices and partialities are known; and must therefore please, if not by favouring them, by forbearing to oppose them. To charge those favourable representations, which men give of their own minds, with the guilt of hypocritical falsehood, would show more severity than knowledge. The writer commonly believes himself. Almost every man's thoughts, while they are general, are right; and most hearts are pure while temptation is away. It is easy to awaken generous sentiments in privacy; to despise death when there is no danger; to glow with benevolence when there is nothing to be given. While such ideas are formed they are felt; and self- love does not suspect the gleam of virtue to be the meteor of fancy.

If the Letters of Pope are considered merely as compositions, they seem to be premeditated and artificial. It is one thing to write because there is something which the mind wishes to discharge, and another to solicit the imagination because ceremony or vanity requires something to be written. Pope confesses his early Letters to be vitiated with AFFECTATION AND AMBITION: to know whether he disentangled himself from these perverters of epistolary integrity, his book and his life must be set in comparison. One of his favourite topics is contempt of his own poetry. For this, if it had been real, he would deserve no commendation; and in this he was certainly not sincere, for his high value of himself was sufficiently observed; and of what could he be proud but of his poetry? He writes, he says, when "he has just nothing else to do;" yet Swift complains that he was never at leisure for conversation, because he "had always some poetical scheme in his head." It was punctually required that his writing-box should be set upon his bed before he rose; and Lord Oxford's domestic related that, in the dreadful winter of Forty, she was called from her bed by him four times in one night, to supply him with paper, lest he should lose a thought. He pretends insensibility to censure and criticism, though it was observed by all who knew him that every pamphlet disturbed his quiet, and that his extreme irritability laid him open to perpetual vexation; but he wished to despise his critics, and therefore hoped that he did despise them. As he happened to live in two reigns when the court paid little attention to poetry, he nursed in his mind a foolish disesteem of kings, and proclaims that "he never sees courts." Yet a little regard shown him by the Prince of Wales melted his obduracy; and he had not much to say when he was asked by his Royal Highness, "How he could love a prince while he disliked kings?"

He very frequently professes contempt of the world, and represents himself as looking on mankind, sometimes with gay indifference, as on emmets of a hillock, below his serious attention; and sometimes with gloomy indignation, as on monsters more worthy of hatred than pity. These were dispositions apparently counterfeited. How could he despise those whom he lived by pleasing, and on whose approbation his esteem of himself was superstructed? Why should he hate those to whose favour he owed his honour and his ease? Of things that terminate in human life, the world is the proper judge: to despise its sentence, if it were possible, is not just; and if it were just, is not possible. Pope was far enough from this unreasonable temper; he was sufficiently A FOOL TO FAME, and his fault was that he pretended to neglect it. His levity and his sullenness were only in his letters; he passed through common life, sometimes vexed, and sometimes pleased, with the natural emotions of common men. His scorn of the great is repeated too often to be real; no man thinks much of that which he despises; and as falsehood is always in danger of inconsistency, he makes it his boast at another time that he lives among them. It is evident that his own importance swells often in his mind. He is afraid of writing, lest the clerks of the post-office should know his secrets; he has many enemies; he considers himself as surrounded by universal jealousy: "After many deaths, and many dispersions, two or three of us," says he, "may still be brought together, not to plot, but to divert ourselves, and the world too, if it pleases;" and they can live together, and "show what friends wits may be, in spite of all the fools in the world." All this while it was likely that the clerks did not know his hand; he certainly had no more enemies than a public character like his inevitably excites; and with what degree of friendship the wits might live, very few were so much fools as ever to inquire. Some part of this pretended discontent he learned from Swift, and expresses it, I think, most frequently in his correspondence with him. Swift's resentment was unreasonable, but it was sincere; Pope's was the mere mimicry of his friend, a fictitious part which he began to play before it became him. When he was only twenty-five years old, he related that "a glut of study and retirement had thrown him on the world," and that there was danger lest "a glut of the world should throw him back upon study and retirement." To this Swift answered with great propriety, that Pope had not yet acted or suffered enough in the world to have become weary of it. And, indeed, it must have been some very powerful reason that can drive back to solitude him who has once enjoyed the pleasures of society.

In the Letters both of Swift and Pope there appears such narrowness of mind as makes them insensible of any excellence that has not some affinity with their own, and confines their esteem and approbation to so small a number, that whoever should form his opinion of their age from their representation, would suppose them to have lived amidst ignorance and barbarity, unable to find among their contemporaries either virtue or intelligence, and persecuted by those that could not understand them.

When Pope murmurs at the world, when he professes contempt of fame, when he speaks of riches and poverty, of success and disappointment, with negligent indifference, he certainly does not express his habitual and settled resentments, but either wilfully disguises his own character, or, what is more likely, invests himself with temporary qualities, and sallies out in the colours of the present moment. His hopes and fears, his joys and sorrows, acted strongly upon his mind, and if he differed from others it was not by carelessness; he was irritable and resentful; his malignity to Philips, whom he had first made ridiculous and then hated for being angry continued too long. Of his vain desire to make Bentley contemptible I never heard any adequate reason. He was sometimes wanton in his attacks, and before Chandos, Lady Wortley, and Hill, was mean in his retreat. The virtues which seem to have had most of his affection were liberality and fidelity of friendship, in which it does not appear that he was other than he describes himself. His fortune did not suffer his character to be splendid and conspicuous, but he assisted Dodsley with a hundred pounds that he might open a shop, and of the subscription of forty pounds a year that he raised for Savage twenty were paid by himself. He was accused of loving money, but his love was eagerness to gain, not solicitude to keep it. In the duties of friendship he was zealous and constant; his early maturity of mind commonly united him with men older than himself, and therefore, without attaining any considerable length of life, he saw many companions of his youth sink into the grave; but it does not appear that he lost a single friend by coldness or by injury; those who loved him once continued their kindness. His ungrateful mention of Allen in his will was the effect of his adherence to one whom he had known much longer, and whom he naturally loved with greater fondness. His violation of the trust reposed in him by Bolingbroke could have no motive inconsistent with the warmest affection; he either thought the action so near to indifferent that he forgot it, or so laudable that he expected his friend to approve it. It was reported with such confidence as almost to enforce belief, that in the papers entrusted to his executors was found a defamatory Life of Swift, which he had prepared as an instrument of vengeance, to be used if any provocation should be ever given. About this I inquired of the Earl of Marchmont, who assured me that no such piece was among his remains.

The religion in which he lived and died was that of the Church of Rome, to which, in his correspondence with Racine, he professes himself a sincere adherent. That he was not scrupulously pious in some part of his life is known by many idle and indecent applications of sentences taken from the Scriptures, a mode of merriment which a good man dreads for its profaneness, and a witty man disdains for its easiness and vulgarity. But to whatever levities he has been betrayed, it does not appear that his principles were ever corrupted, or that he ever lost his belief of revelation. The positions which he transmitted from Bolingbroke he seems not to have understood, and was pleased with an interpretation that made them orthodox.

A man of such exalted superiority and so little moderation would naturally have all his delinquencies observed and aggravated; those who could not deny that he was excellent would rejoice to find that he was not perfect. Perhaps it may be imputed to the unwillingness with which the same man is allowed to possess many advantages, that his learning has been depreciated. He certainly was in his early life a man of great literary curiosity, and when he wrote his "Essay on Criticism," had, for his age, a very wide acquaintance with books. When he entered into the living world it seems to have happened to him, as to many others, that he was less attentive to dead masters; he studied in the academy of Paracelsus, and made the universe his favourite volume. He gathered his notions fresh from reality, not from the copies of authors, but the originals of Nature. Yet there is no reason to believe that literature ever lost his esteem; he always professed to love reading, and Dobson, who spent some time at his house translating his "Essay on Man," when I asked him what learning he found him to possess, answered, "More than I expected." His frequent references to history, his allusions to various kinds of knowledge, and his images selected from art and nature, with his observations on the operations of the mind and the modes of life, show an intelligence perpetually on the wing, excursive, vigorous, and diligent, eager to pursue knowledge, and attentive to retain it.

From this curiosity arose the desire of travelling, to which he alludes in his verses to Jervas, and which, though he never found an opportunity to gratify it, did not leave him till his life declined.

Of his intellectual character, the constituent and fundamental principle was good sense, a prompt and intuitive perception of consonance and propriety. He saw immediately of his own conceptions what was to be chosen and what to be rejected, and, in the works of others, what was to be shunned and what to be copied. But good sense alone is a sedate and quiescent quality, which manages its possessions well, but does not increase them; it collects few materials for its own operations, and preserves safety, but never gains supremacy. Pope had likewise genius; a mind active, ambitious, and adventurous, always investigating, always aspiring; in its widest searches still longing to go forward, in its highest flights still wishing to be higher, always imagining some thing greater than it knows, always endeavouring more than it can do. To assist these powers he is said to have had great strength and exactness of memory. That which he had heard or read was not easily lost, and he had before him not only what his own meditations suggested, but what he had found in other writers that might be accommodated to his present purpose. These benefits of Nature he improved by incessant and unwearied diligence; he had recourse to every source of intelligence, and lost no opportunity of information; he consulted the living as well as the dead; he read his compositions to his friends, and was never content with mediocrity when excellence could be attained. He considered poetry as the business of his life, and however he might seem to lament his occupation he followed it with constancy; to make verses was his first labour, and to mend them was his last. From his attention to poetry he was never diverted. If conversation offered anything that could be improved, he committed it to paper; if a thought, or perhaps an expression, more happy than was common, rose to his mind, he was careful to write it; an independent distich was preserved for an opportunity of insertion, and some little fragments have been found containing lines, or parts of lines, to be wrought upon at some other time. He was one of those few whose labour is their pleasure; he was never elevated to negligence nor wearied to impatience; he never passed a fault unamended by indifference, nor quitted it by despair. He laboured his works first to gain reputation, and afterwards to keep it.

Of composition there are different methods. Some employ at once memory and invention, and, with little intermediate use of the pen, form and polish large masses by continued meditation, and write their productions only when, in their own opinion, they have completed them. It is related of Virgil that his custom was to pour out a great number of verses in the morning, and pass the day in retrenching exuberances and correcting inaccuracies. The method of Pope, as may be collected from his translation, was to write his first thoughts in his first words, and gradually to amplify, decorate, rectify, and refine them. With such faculties and such dispositions he excelled every other writer in poetical prudence; he wrote in such a manner as might expose him to few hazards. He used almost always the same fabric of verse, and, indeed, by those few essays which he made of any other, he did not enlarge his reputation. Of this uniformity the certain consequence was readiness and dexterity. By perpetual practice language had, in his mind, a systematical arrangement; having always the same use for words, he had words so selected and combined as to be ready at his call. This increase of facility he confessed himself to have perceived in the progress of his translation. But what was yet of more importance, his effusions were always voluntary, and his subjects chosen by himself. His independence secured him from drudging at a task, and labouring upon a barren topic; he never exchanged praise for money, nor opened a shop of condolence or congratulation. His poems, therefore, were scarcely ever temporary. He suffered coronations and royal marriages to pass without a song, and derived no opportunities from recent events, nor any popularity from the accidental disposition of his readers. He was never reduced to the necessity of soliciting the sun to shine upon a birthday, of calling the graces and virtues to a wedding, or of saying what multitudes have said before him. When he could produce nothing new he was at liberty to be silent.

His publications were for the same reason never hasty. He is said to have sent nothing to the press till it had lain two years under his inspection: it is at least certain that he ventured nothing without nice examination. He suffered the tumult of imagination to subside, and the novelties of invention to grow familiar. He knew that the mind is always enamoured of its own productions, and did not trust his first fondness. He consulted his friends, and listened with great willingness to criticism; and, what was of more importance, he consulted himself, and let nothing pass against his own judgment. He professed to have learned his poetry from Dryden, whom, whenever an opportunity was presented, he praised through his whole life with unvaried liberality; and perhaps his character may receive some illustration if he be compared with his master.

Integrity of understanding and nicety of discernment were not allotted in a less proportion to Dryden than to Pope. The rectitude of Dryden's mind was sufficiently shown by the dismission of his poetical prejudices, and the rejection of unnatural thoughts and rugged numbers. But Dryden never desired to apply all the judgment that he had. He wrote, and professed to write, merely for the people; and when he pleased others, he contented himself. He spent no time in struggles to rouse latent powers; he never attempted to make that better which was already good, nor often to mend what he must have known to be faulty. He wrote, as he tells us, with very little consideration; when occasion or necessity called upon him, he poured out what the present moment happened to supply, and, when once it had passed the press, ejected it from his mind; for, when he had no pecuniary interest, he had no further solicitude.

Pope was not content to satisfy; he desired to excel, and therefore always endeavoured to do his best; he did not court the candour, but dared the judgment of his reader, and, expecting no indulgence from others, he showed none to himself. He examined lines and words with minute and punctilious observation, and retouched every part with indefatigable diligence, till he had left nothing to be forgiven. For this reason he kept his pieces very long in his hands, while he considered and reconsidered them. The only poems which can be supposed to have been written with such regard to the times as might hasten their publication, were the two satires of "Thirty-eight;" of which Dodsley told me that they were brought to him by the author, that they might be fairly copied. "Almost every line," he said, "was then written twice over; I gave him a clean transcript, which he sent some time afterwards to me for the press, with almost every line written twice over a second time." His declaration, that his care for his works ceased at their publication, was not strictly true. His parental attention never abandoned them; what he found amiss in the first edition, he silently corrected in those that followed. He appears to have revised the "Iliad," and freed it from some of its imperfections; and the "Essay on Criticism" received many improvements after its first appearance. It will seldom be found that he altered without adding clearness, elegance, or vigour.

Pope had perhaps the judgment of Dryden; but Dryden certainly wanted the diligence of Pope.

In acquired knowledge, the superiority must be allowed to Dryden, whose education was more scholastic, and who before he became an author had been allowed more time for study, with better means of information. His mind has a larger range, and he collects his images and illustrations from a more extensive circumference of science. Dryden knew more of man in his general nature, and Pope in his local manners. The notions of Dryden were formed by comprehensive speculation, and those of Pope by minute attention. There is more dignity in the knowledge of Dryden, and more certainty in that of Pope. Poetry was not the sole praise of either; for both excelled likewise in prose; but Pope did not borrow his prose from his predecessor. The style of Dryden is capricious and varied; that of Pope is cautious and uniform. Dryden observes the motions of his own mind; Pope constrains his mind to his own rules of composition. Dryden is sometimes vehement and rapid; Pope is always smooth, uniform, and gentle. Dryden's page is a natural field, rising into inequalities, and diversified by the varied exuberance of abundant vegetation; Pope's is a velvet lawn, shaven by the scythe, and levelled by the roller.

Of genius, that power which constitutes a poet; that quality without which judgment is cold, and knowledge is inert; that energy which collects, combines, amplifies, and animates; the superiority must, with some hesitation, be allowed to Dryden. It is not to be inferred that of this poetical vigour Pope had only a little, because Dryden had more; for every other writer since Milton must give place to Pope; and even of Dryden it must be said that, if he has brighter paragraphs, he has not better poems. Dryden's performances were always hasty, either excited by some external occasion, or extorted by domestic necessity; he composed without consideration, and published without correction. What his mind could supply at call, or gather in one excursion, was all that he sought, and all that he gave. The dilatory caution of Pope enabled him to condense his sentiments, to multiply his images, and to accumulate all that study might produce or chance might supply. If the flights of Dryden therefore are higher, Pope continues longer on the wing. If of Dryden's fire the blaze is brighter, of Pope's the heat is more regular and constant. Dryden often surpasses expectation, and Pope never falls below it. Dryden is read with frequent astonishment, and Pope with perpetual delight. This parallel will, I hope, when it is well considered, be found just; and if the reader should suspect me, as I suspect myself, of some partial fondness for the memory of Dryden, let him not too hastily condemn me; for meditation and inquiry may, perhaps, show him the reasonableness of my determination.

The Works of Pope are now to be distinctly examined, not so much with attention to slight faults or petty beauties, as to the general character and effect of each performance.

It seems natural for a young poet to initiate himself by pastorals, which, not professing to imitate real life, require no experience; and, exhibiting only the simple operation of unmingled passions, admit no subtle reasoning or deep inquiry. Pope's pastorals are not, however, composed but with close thought; they have reference to the times of the day, the seasons of the year, and the periods of human life. The last, that which turns the attention upon age and death, was the author's favourite. To tell of disappointment and misery, to thicken the darkness of futurity and perplex the labyrinth of uncertainty, has been always a delicious employment of the poets. His preference was probably just. I wish, however, that his fondness had not overlooked a line in which the Zephyrs are made to lament in silence. To charge these pastorals with wane of invention, is to require what was never intended. The imitations are so ambitiously frequent, that the writer evidently means rather to show his literature than his wit. It is surely sufficient for an author of sixteen, not only to be able to copy the poems of antiquity with judicious selection, but to have obtained sufficient power of language, and skill in metre, to exhibit a series of versification which had in English poetry no precedent, nor has since had an imitation.

The design of "Windsor Forest" is evidently derived from "Cooper's Hill," with some attention to Waller's poem on "The Park;" but Pope cannot be denied to excel his masters in variety and elegance, and the art of interchanging description, narrative, and morality. The objection made by Dennis is the want of plan, of a regular subordination of parts terminating in the principal and original design. There is this want in most descriptive poems, because as the scenes, which they must exhibit successively, are all subsisting at the same time, the order in which they are shown must by necessity be arbitrary, and more is not to be expected from the last part than from the first. The attention, therefore, which cannot be detained by suspense, must be excited by diversity, such as this poem offers to its reader. But the desire of diversity may be too much indulged; the parts of "Windsor Forest" which deserve least praise are those which were added to enliven the stillness of the scene--the appearance of Father Thames, and the transformation of Lodona. Addison had in his "Campaign" derided the rivers that "rise from their oozy beds" to tell stories of heroes; and it is therefore strange that Pope should adopt a fiction not only un-natural, but lately censured. The story of Lodona is told with sweetness; but a new metamorphosis is a ready and puerile expedient; nothing is easier than to tell how a flower was once a blooming virgin, or a rock an obdurate tyrant.

The "Temple of Fame" has, as Steele warmly declared, a "thousand beauties." Every part is splendid; there is great luxuriance of ornaments; the original vision of Chaucer was never denied to be much improved; the allegory is very skilfully con-tinued, the imagery is properly selected, and learnedly displayed; yet, with all this comprehension of excellence, as its scene is laid in remote ages, and its sentiments, if the concluding paragraph be excepted, have little relation to general manners or common life, it never obtained much notice, but is turned silently over, and seldom quoted or mentioned with either praise or blame.

That the "Messiah" excels the "Pollio" is no great praise, if it be considered from what original the improvements are derived.

The "Verses on the Unfortunate Lady" have drawn much attention by the il-laudable singularity of treating suicide with respect; and they must be allowed to be written in some parts with vigorous animation, and in others with gentle tender-ness; nor has Pope produced any poem in which the sense predominates more over the diction. But the tale is not skilfully told; it is not easy to discover the character of either the lady or her guardian. History relates that she was about to disparage herself by a marriage with an inferior; Pope praises her for the dignity of ambition, and yet condemns the uncle to detestation for his pride; the ambitious love of a niece may be opposed by the interest, malice, or envy of an uncle, but never by his pride. On such an occasion a poet may be allowed to be obscure, but inconsistency never can be right.

The "Ode for St. Cecilia's Day" was undertaken at the desire of Steele: in this the author is generally confessed to have miscarried, yet he has miscarried only as compared with Dryden; for he has far outgone other competitors. Dryden's plan is better chosen; history will always take stronger hold of the attention than fable:

the passions excited by Dryden are the pleasures and pains of real life, the scene of Pope is laid in imaginary existence; Pope is read with calm acquiescence, Dryden with turbulent delight; Pope hangs upon the ear, and Dryden finds the passes of the mind. Both the odes want the essential constituent of metrical compositions, the stated recurrence of settled numbers. It may be alleged that Pindar is said by Horace to have written numeris lege solutis; but as no such lax performances have been transmitted to us, the meaning of that expression cannot be fixed; and perhaps the like return might properly be made to a modern Pindarist as Mr. Cobb received from Bentley, who, when he found his criticisms upon a Greek exercise, which Cobb had presented, refuted one after another by Pindar's authority, cried out at last, "Pindar was a bold fellow, but thou art an impudent one."

If Pope's ode be particularly inspected, it will be found that the first stanza consists of sounds well chosen indeed, but only sounds. The second consists of hyperbolical commonplaces, easily to be found, and perhaps without much difficulty to be as well expressed. In the third, however, there are numbers, images, harmony, and rigour, not unworthy the antagonist of Dryden. Had all been like this--but every part cannot be the best. The next stanzas place and detain us in the dark and dismal regions of mythology, where neither hope nor fear, neither joy nor sorrow can be found: the poet, however, faithfully attends us; we have all that can be performed by elegance of diction or sweetness of versification; but what can form avail without better matter? The last stanza recurs again to commonplaces. The conclusion is too evidently modelled by that of Dryden; and it may be remarked that both end with the same fault; the comparison of each is literal on one side and metaphorical on the other. Poets do not always express their own thoughts: Pope, with all this labour in the praise of music, was ignorant of its principles and insensible of its effects.

One of his greatest, though of his earliest works, is the "Essay on Criticism," which, if he had written nothing else, would have placed him among the first critics and the first poets, as it exhibits every mode of excellence that can embellish or dignify didactic composition, selection of matter, novelty of arrangement, justness of precept, splendour of illustration, and propriety of digression. I know not whether it be pleasing to consider that he produced this piece at twenty, and never afterwards excelled it: he that delights himself with observing that such powers may be soon attained, cannot but grieve to think that life was ever after at a stand.

To mention the particular beauties of the essay would be unprofitably tedious: but I cannot forbear to observe that the comparison of a student's progress in the sciences with the journey of a traveller in the Alps is perhaps the best that English poetry can show. A simile, to be perfect, must both illustrate and ennoble the subject; must show it to the understanding in a clearer view, and display it to the fancy with greater dignity; but either of these qualities may be sufficient to recommend it. In didactic poetry, of which the great purpose is instruction, a simile may be praised which illustrates, though it does not ennoble; in heroics, that may be admitted which ennobles, though it does not illustrate. That it may be complete, it is required to exhibit, independently of its references, a pleasing image; for a simile is said to be a short episode. To this antiquity was so attentive, that circumstances were sometimes added, which, having no parallels, served only to fill the imagination, and produced what Perrault ludicrously called "comparisons with a long tail." In their similes the greatest writers have sometimes failed; the ship-race, compared with the chariot-race, is neither illustrated nor aggrandised; land and water make all the difference: when Apollo, running after Daphne, is likened to a greyhound chasing a hare, there is nothing gained; the ideas of pursuit and flight are too plain to be made plainer; and a god and the daughter of a god are not represented much to their advantage by a hare and dog. The simile of the Alps has no useless parts, yet affords a striking picture by itself; it makes the foregoing position better understood, and enables it to take faster hold on the attention; it assists the apprehension and elevates the fancy. Let me likewise dwell a little on the celebrated paragraph in which it is directed that "the sound should seem an echo to the sense;" a precept which Pope is allowed to have observed beyond any other English poet.

This notion of representative metre, and the desire of discovering frequent adaptations of the sound to the sense, have produced, in my opinion, many wild conceits and imaginary beauties. All that can furnish this representation are the sounds of the words considered singly and the time in which they are pronounced. Every language has some words framed to exhibit the noises which they express, as THUMP, RATTLE, GROWL, HISS. These, however, are but few, and the poet cannot make them more, nor can they be of any use but when sound is to be mentioned. The time of pronunciation was in the dactylic measures of the learned languages capable of considerable variety; but that variety could be accommodated only to motion or duration, and different degrees of motion were perhaps expressed by verses rapid or slow, without much attention of the writer, when the image had full possession of his fancy: but our language having little flexibility, our verses can differ very little in their cadence. The fancied resemblances, I fear, arise sometimes merely from the ambiguity of words; there is supposed to be some relation between a SOFT line and SOFT couch, or between HEARD syllables and HARD fortune. Motion, however, may be in some sort exemplified; and yet it may be suspected that in such resemblances the mind often governs the ear, and the sounds are estimated by their meaning. One of their most successful attempts has been to describe the labour of Sisyphus:-

"With many a weary step, and many a groan, Up a high hill he heaves a huge round stone; The huge round stone, resulting with a bound, Thunders impetuous down, and smokes along the ground."

Who does not perceive the stone to move slowly upward, and roll violently back? But set the same numbers to another sense:-

"While many a merry tale, and many a song, Cheered the rough road, we wished the rough road long. The rough road, then, returning in a round, Mocked our impatient steps, for all was fairy ground."

We have now surely lost much of the delay and much of the rapidity. But, to show how little the greatest master of numbers can fix the principles of representative harmony, it will be sufficient to remark that the poet who tells us that -

"When Ajax strives some rock's vast weight to throw, The line too labours, and the words move slow: Not so when swift Camilla scours the plain, Flies o'er th' unbending corn, and skims along the main;"

when he had enjoyed for about thirty years the praise of Camilla's lightness of foot, he tried another experiment upon SOUND and TIME, and produced this memorable triplet:-

"Waller was smooth; but Dryden taught to join The varying verse, the full resounding line, The long majestic march, and energy divine."

Here are the swiftness of the rapid race, and the march of slow- paced majesty, exhibited by the same poet in the same sequence of syllables, except that the exact prosodist will find the line of SWIFTNESS by one time longer than that of TARDI-

NESS. Beauties of this kind are commonly fancied, and, when real, are technical and nugatory, not to he rejected and not to be solicited.

To the praises which have been accumulated on the "Rape of the Look" by readers of every class, from the critic to the waiting-maid, it is difficult to make any addition. Of that which is universally allowed to be the most attractive of all ludicrous compositions, let it rather be now inquired from what sources the power of pleasing is derived.

Dr. Warburton, who excelled in critical perspicacity, has remarked that the preternatural agents are very happily adapted to the purposes of the poem. The heathen deities can no longer gain attention; we should have turned away from a contest between Venus and Diana. The employment of allegorical persons always excites conviction of its own absurdity; they may produce effects, but cannot conduct actions; when the phantom is put in motion it dissolves; thus Discord may raise a mutiny, but Discord cannot conduct a march nor besiege a town. Pope brought in view a new race of beings, with powers and passions proportionate to their operation. The Sylphs and Gnomes act at the toilet and the tea- table what more terrific and more powerful phantoms perform on the stormy ocean or the field of battle: they give their proper help and do their proper mischief. Pope is said, by an objector, not to have been the inventor of this petty notion, a charge which might with more justice have been brought against the author of the "Iliad," who doubtless adopted the religious system of his country; for what is there but the names of his agents which Pope has not invented? Has he not assigned them characters and operations never heard of before? Has he not, at least, given them their first poetical existence? If this is not sufficient to denominate his work original, nothing original ever can be written.

In this work are exhibited in a very high degree the two most engaging powers of an author. New things are made familiar, and familiar things are made new. A race of aerial people never heard of before is presented to us in a manner so clear and easy that the reader seeks for no further information, but immediately mingles with his new acquaintance, adopts their interests, and attends their pursuits, loves a Sylph, and detests a Gnome. That familiar things are made new every paragraph will prove. The subject of the poem is an event below the common incidents of common life; nothing real is introduced that is not seen so often as to be no longer regarded; yet the whole detail of a female day is here brought before us, invested with so much art of decoration that, though nothing is disguised, everything is striking, and we feel all the appetite of curiosity for that from which we have a thousand times turned fastidiously away.

The purpose of the poet is, as he tells us, to laugh at "the little unguarded follies of the female sex." It is therefore without justice that Dennis charges the "Rape of the Lock" with the want of a moral, and for that reason sets it below the "Lutrin," which exposes the pride and discord of the clergy. Perhaps neither Pope nor Boileau has made the world much better than he found it; but if they had both succeeded, it were easy to tell who would have deserved most from public gratitude. The freaks, and humours, and spleen, and vanity of women as they embroil families in discord, and fill houses with disquiet, do more to obstruct the happiness of life in a year than the ambition of the clergy in many centuries. It has been well observed that the misery of man proceeds not from any single crush of overwhelming evil, but from small vexatious continually repeated. It is remarked by Dennis, likewise, that the machinery is superfluous; that, by all the bustle of preternatural operation, the main event is neither hastened nor retarded. To this charge an efficacious answer is not easily made. The Sylphs cannot be said to help or oppose; and it must be allowed to imply some want of art that their power has not been sufficiently intermingled with the action. Other parts may likewise be charged with want of connection--the game at ombre might be spared; but if the lady had lost her hair while she was intent upon her cards it might have been inferred that those who are too fond of play will be in danger of neglecting more important interests. Those, perhaps, are faults, but what are such faults to so much excellence!

The Epistle of "Eloise to Abelard" is one of the most happy productions of human wit; the subject is so judiciously chosen that it would be difficult in turning over the annals of the world to find another which so many circumstances concur to recommend. We regularly interest ourselves most in the fortune of those who most deserve our notice. Abelard and Eloise were conspicuous in their days for eminence of merit. The heart naturally loves truth. The adventures and misfortunes of this illustrious pair are known from undisputed history. Their fate does not leave the mind in hopeless dejection, for they both found quiet and consolation in retirement and piety. So new and so affecting is their story that it supersedes invention, and imagination ranges at full liberty without straggling into scenes of fable. The story thus skilfully adopted has been diligently improved. Pope has left nothing behind him which seems more the effect of studious perseverance and laborious revisal. Here is particularly observable the curiosa felicitas, a fruitful soil and careful cultivation. Here is no crudeness of sense nor asperity of language. The sources from which sentiments which have so much vigour and efficacy have been drawn are shown to be the mystic writers by the learned author of the "Essays on the Life and Writings of Pope," a book which teaches how the brow of Criticism may be smoothed, and how she may be enabled, with all her severity, to attract and to delight.

The train of my disquisition has now conducted me to that poetical wonder, the translation of the "Iliad," a performance which no age or nation can pretend to equal. To the Greeks translation was almost unknown; it was totally unknown to the inhabitants of Greece. They had no recourse to the barbarians for poetical beauties, but sought for everything in Homer, where, indeed, there is but little which they might not find. The Italians have been very diligent translators, but I can hear of no version, unless, perhaps, Anguillara's "Ovid" may be excepted, which is read with eagerness. The "Iliad" of Salvini every reader may discover to be punctiliously exact; but it seems to be the work of a linguist skilfully pedantic; and his countrymen, the proper judges of its power to please, reject it with disgust. Their predecessors, the Romans, have left some specimens of translation behind them, and that employment must have had some credit in which Tully and Germanicus engaged; but unless we suppose, what is perhaps true, that the plays of Terence were versions of Menander, nothing translated seems ever to have risen to high reputation. The French in the meridian hour of their learning were very laudably industrious to enrich their own language with the wisdom of the ancients; but found themselves reduced by whatever necessity to turn the Greek and Roman poetry into prose. Whoever could read an author could translate him. From such rivals little can be feared.

The chief help of Pope in this audacious undertaking was drawn from the versions of Dryden. Virgil had borrowed much of his imagery from Homer; and part of the debt was now paid by his translator. Pope searched the pages of Dryden for happy combinations of heroic diction, but it will not be denied that he added much to what he found. He cultivated our language with so much diligence and art, that he has left in his "Homer" a treasure of poetical elegances to posterity. His version may be said to have tuned the English tongue; for since its appearance no writer, however deficient in other powers, has wanted melody. Such a series of lines, so elaborately corrected, and so sweetly modulated, took possession of the public ear; the vulgar was enamoured of the poem, and the learned wondered at the translation. But in the most general applause discordant voices will always be heard. It has been objected by some who wish to be numbered among the sons of learning that Pope's version of Homer is not Homerical; that it exhibits no resemblance of the original and characteristic manner of the Father of Poetry, as it wants his artless grandeur, his unaffected majesty. This cannot be totally denied; but it must be remembered that necessitas quod cogit defendit; that may be lawfully done which cannot be forborne. Time and place will always enforce regard. In estimating this translation, consideration must be had of the nature of our language, the form of our metre, and, above all, of the change which two thousand years have made in the modes of life and the habits of thought. Virgil wrote in a language of the same general fabric with that of Homer, in verses of the same measure, and in an age nearer to Homer's time by eighteen hundred years; yet he found even then the state of the world so much altered, and the demand for elegance so much increased, that mere nature would be endured no longer; and, perhaps, in the multitude of borrowed passages, very few can be shown which he has not embellished.

There is a time when nations, emerging from barbarity, and falling into regular subordination, gain leisure to grow wise, and feel the shame of ignorance and the craving pain of unsatisfied curiosity. To this hunger of the mind plain sense is grateful; that which fills the void removes uneasiness, and to be free from pain for a while is pleasure; but repletion generates fastidiousness; a saturated intellect soon becomes luxurious, and knowledge finds no willing reception till it is recommended by artificial diction. Thus it will be found, in the progress of learning, that in all nations the first writers are simple, and that every age improves in elegance. One refinement always makes way for another; and what was expedient to Virgil was necessary to Pope. I suppose many readers of the English "Iliad," when they have been touched with some unexpected beauty of the lighter kind, have tried to enjoy it in the original, where, alas! it was not to be found. Homer doubtless owes to his translator many Ovidian graces not exactly suitable to his character; but to have added can be no great crime, if nothing be taken away. Elegance is surely to be desired, if it be not gained at the expense of dignity. A hero would wish to be loved, as well as to be reverenced. To a thousand cavils one answer is sufficient; the purpose of a writer is to be read, and the criticism which would destroy the power of pleasing must be blown aside. Pope wrote for his own age and his own nation: he knew that it was necessary to colour the images and point the sentiments of his author; he therefore made him graceful, but lost him some of his sublimity. The copious notes with which the version is accompanied, and by which it is recommended to many readers, though they were undoubtedly written to swell the volumes, ought not to pass without praise: commentaries which attract the reader by the pleasure of perusal have not often appeared; the notes of others are read to clear difficulties; those of Pope to vary entertainment. It has, however, been objected, with sufficient reason, that there is in the commentary too much of unseasonable levity and affected gaiety; that too many appeals are made to the ladies, and the ease which is so carefully preserved is sometimes the ease of a trifler. Every art has its terms, and every kind of instruction its proper style; the gravity of common critics may be tedious, but is less despicable than childish merriment.

Of the "Odyssey" nothing remains to be observed; the same general praise may be given to both translations, and a particular examination of either would require a large volume. The notes were written by Broome, who endeavoured, not unsuccessfully, to imitate his master.

Of the "Dunciad" the hint is confessedly taken from Dryden's "Mac Flecknoe;" but the plan is so enlarged and diversified as justly to claim the praise of an original, and affords the best specimen that has yet appeared of personal satire ludicrously pompous. That the design was moral, whatever the author might tell either his readers or himself, I am not convinced. The first motive was the desire of revenging the contempt with which Theobald had treated his Shakspeare, and regaining the honour which he had lost, by crushing his opponent. Theobald was not of bulk enough to fill a poem, and therefore it was necessary to find other enemies with other names, at whose expense he might divert the public.

In this design there was petulance and malignity enough; but I cannot think it very criminal. An author places himself uncalled before the tribunal of criticism, and solicits fame at the hazard of disgrace. Dulness or deformity are not culpable in themselves, but may be very justly reproached when they pretend to the honour of wit or the influence of beauty. If bad writers were to pass without reprehension, what should restrain them? impune diem consumpserit ingens Telephus; and upon bad writers only will censure have much effect. The satire which brought Theobald and Moore into contempt dropped impotent from Bentley, like the javelin of Priam. All truth is valuable, and satirical criticism may be considered as useful when it rectifies error and improves judgment; he that refines the public taste is a public benefactor. The beauties of this poem are well known; its chief fault is the grossness of its images. Pope and Swift had an unnatural delight in ideas physically impure, such as every other tongue utters with unwillingness, and of which every ear shrinks from the mention. But even this fault, offensive as it is, may be forgiven for the excellence of other passages; such as the formation and dissolution of Moore, the account of the Traveller, the misfortune of the Florist, and the crowded thoughts and stately numbers which dignify the concluding paragraph. The alterations which have been made in the "Dunciad," not always for the better, require that it should be published, as in the present collection, with all its variations.

The "Essay on Man" was a work of great labour and long consideration, but certainly not the happiest of Pope's performances. The subject is perhaps not very proper for poetry; and the poet was not sufficiently master of his subject; metaphysical morality was to him a new study; he was proud of his acquisitions, and, supposing himself master of great secrets, was in haste to teach what he had not learned. Thus he tells us, in the first Epistle, that from the nature of the Supreme Being may be deduced an order of beings such as mankind, because infinite excellence can do only what is best. He finds out that these beings must be "somewhere;" and that "all the question is, whether man be in a wrong place." Surely if, according to the poet's Leibnitzian reasoning, we may infer that man ought to be, only because he is, we may allow that his place is the right place, because he has it. Supreme Wisdom is not less infallible in disposing than in creating. But what is meant by SOMEWHERE, and PLACE, and WRONG PIECE, it had been in vain to ask Pope, who probably had never asked himself.

Having exalted himself into the chair of wisdom, he tells us much that every man knows, and much that he does not know himself; that we see but little, and that the order of the universe is beyond our comprehension; an opinion not very uncommon; and that there is a chain of subordinate beings "from infinite to nothing," of which himself and his readers are equally ignorant. But he gives us one comfort, which without his help he supposes unattainable, in the position "that though we are fools, yet God is wise."

This essay affords an egregious instance of the predominance of genius, the dazzling splendour of imagery, and the seductive powers of eloquence. Never was penury of knowledge and vulgarity of sentiment so happily disguised. The reader feels his mind full, though he learns nothing; and, when he meets it in its new array, no longer knows the talk of his mother and his nurse. When these wonder-working sounds sink into sense, and the doctrine of the essay, disrobed of its ornaments, is left to the powers of its naked excellence, what shall we discover? That we are, in comparison with our Creator, very weak and ignorant; that we do not uphold the chain of existence; and that we could not make one another with more skill than we are made. We may learn yet more that the arts of human life were copied from the instinctive operations of other animals; that if the world be made for man, it may be said that man was made for geese. To these profound principles of natural knowledge are added some moral instructions equally new; that self-interest, well understood, will produce social concord; that men are mutual gainers by mutual benefits; that evil is sometimes balanced by good; that human advantages are unstable and fallacious, of uncertain duration and doubtful effect; that our true honour is not to have a great part, but to act it well; that virtue only is our own; and that happiness is always in our power. Surely a man of no very comprehensive search may venture to say that he has heard all this before; but it was never till now recommended by such a blaze of embellishments, or such sweetness of melody. The vigorous contraction of some thoughts, the luxuriant amplification of others, the incidental illustrations, and sometimes the dignity, sometimes the softness of the verses, enchain philosophy, suspend criticism, and oppress judgment by overpowering pleasure. This is true of many paragraphs; yet, if I had undertaken to exemplify Pope's felicity of composition before a rigid critic, I should not select the "Essay on Man;" for it contains more lines unsuccessfully laboured, more harshness of diction, and more thoughts imperfectly expressed, more levity without elegance, and more heaviness without strength, than will easily be found in all his other works.

The "Characters of Men and Women" are the product of diligent speculation upon human life; much labour has been bestowed upon them, and Pope very seldom laboured in vain. That his excellence may be properly estimated, I recommend a comparison of his "Characters of Women" with Boileau's Satire; it will then be seen with how much more perspicacity female nature is investigated, and female excellence selected; and he surely is no mean writer to whom Boileau should be found inferior. The "Characters of Men," however, are written with more, if not with deeper, thought, and exhibit many passages exquisitely beautiful. The "Gem and the Flower" will not easily be equalled. In the women's part are some defects; the character of Atossa is not so neatly finished as that of Clodio, and some of the female characters may be found, perhaps, more frequently among men; what is said of Philomede was true of Prior.

In the Epistles to Lord Bathurst and Lord Burlington, Dr. Warburton has endeavoured to find a train of thought which was never in the writer's head, and, to support his hypothesis, has printed that first which was published last. In one the most valuable passage is perhaps the Elegy on Good Sense, and the other the end of the Duke of Buckingham.

The Epistle to Arbuthnot, now arbitrarily called the "Prologue to the Satires," is a performance consisting, as it seems, of many fragments wrought into one design, which, by this union of scattered beauties, contains more striking paragraphs than could probably have been brought together into an occasional work. As there is no stronger motive to exertion than self-defence, no part has more elegance, spirit, or dignity, than the poet's vindication of his own character. The meanest passage is the satire upon Sporus.

Of the two poems which derived their names from the year, and which are called the "Epilogue to the Satires," it was very justly remarked by Savage that the second was in the whole more strongly conceived, and more equally supported, but that it had no single passages equal to the contention in the first for the dignity of Vice and the celebration of the triumph of Corruption.

The "Imitations of Horace" seem to have been written as relaxations of his genius. This employment became his favourite by its facility; the plan was ready to his hand, and nothing was required but to accommodate as he could the sentiments of an old author to recent facts or familiar images; but what is easy is seldom excellent. Such imitations cannot give pleasure to common readers; the man of learning may be sometimes surprised and delighted by an unexpected parallel, but the comparison requires knowledge of the original, which will likewise often detect strained applications. Between Roman images and English manners there will be an irreconcilable dissimilitude, and the works will be generally uncouth and particoloured, neither original nor translated, neither ancient nor modern.

Pope had, in proportions very nicely adjusted to each other, all the qualities that constitute genius. He had INTENTION, by which new trains of events are formed and new scenes of imagery displayed, as in the "Rape of the Lock," and by which extrinsic and adventitious embellishments and illustrations are connected with a known subject, as in the "Essay on Criticism." He had IMAGINATION, which strongly impresses on the writer's mind, and enables him to convey to the reader the various forms of nature, incidents of life, and energies of passion, as in his "Eloisa," "Windsor Forest," and "Ethic Epistles." He had JUDGMENT, which selects from life or Nature what the present purpose requires, and by separating the essence of things from its concomitants, often makes the representation more powerful than the reality; and he had colours of language always before him, ready to decorate his matter with every grace of elegant expression, as when he accommodates his diction to the wonderful multiplicity of Homer's sentiments and descriptions.

Poetical expression includes sound as well as meaning. "Music," says Dryden, "is inarticulate poetry;" among the excellences of Pope, therefore, must be mentioned the melody of his metre. By perusing the works of Dryden, he discovered the most perfect fabric of English verse, and habituated himself to that only which he found the best; in consequence of which restraint his poetry has been censured as too uniformly musical, and as glutting the ear with unvaried sweetness. I suspect this objection to be the cant of those who judge by principles rather than perception, and who would even themselves have less pleasure in his works if he had tried to relieve attention by studied discords, or affected to break his lines and vary his pauses. But though he was thus careful of his versification, he did not oppress his powers with superfluous rigour. He seems to have thought with Boileau that the practice of writing might be refined till the difficulty should overbalance the advantage. The construction of the language is not always strictly grammatical; with those rhymes which prescription had conjoined he contented himself, without regard to Swift's remonstrances, though there was no striking consonance, nor was he very careful to vary his terminations or to refuse admission, at a small distance, to the same rhymes. To Swift's edict for the exclusion of alexandrines and triplets he paid little regard; he admitted them, but, in the opinion of Fenton, too rarely; he uses them more liberally in his translation than his poems. He has a few double rhymes, and always, I think, unsuccessfully, except once in the "Rape of the Lock." Expletives he very early ejected from his verses, but he now and then admits an epithet rather commodious than important. Each of the six first lines of the "Iliad" might lose two syllables with very little diminution of the meaning, and sometimes, after all his art and labour, one verse seems to be made for the sake of another. In his latter productions the diction is sometimes vitiated by French idioms, with which Bolingbroke had perhaps infected him.

I have been told that the couplet by which he declared his own ear to be most gratified was this:-

"Lo, where Maeotis sleeps, and hardly flows The freezing Tanais through a waste of snows."

But the reason of this preference I cannot discover.

It is remarked by Watts that there is scarcely a happy combination of words, or a phrase poetically elegant in the English language, which Pope has not inserted into his version of Homer. How he obtained possession of so many beauties of speech it were desirable to know. That he gleaned from authors, obscure as well as eminent, what he thought brilliant or useful, and preserved it all in a regular collection, is not unlikely. When, in his last years, Hall's "Satires" were shown him, he wished that he had seen them sooner. New sentiments and new images others may produce; but to attempt any further improvement of versification will be dangerous. Art and diligence have now done their best, and what shall be added will be the effort of tedious toil and needless curiosity. After all this, it is surely superfluous to answer the question that has once been asked, Whether Pope was a poet, otherwise than by asking in return, If Pope be not a poet, where is poetry to be found? To circumscribe poetry by a definition will only show the narrowness of the definer, though a definition which shall exclude Pope will not easily be made. Let us look round upon the present time and back upon the past; let us inquire to whom the voice of mankind has decreed the wreath of poetry; let their productions be examined, and their claims stated, and the pretensions of Pope will be no more disputed. Had he given the world only his version, the name of poet must have been allowed him: if the writer of the "Iliad" were to class his successors he would assign a very high place to his translator, without requiring any other evidence of genius.

The following letter, of which the original is in the hands of Lord Hardwicke, was communicated to me by the kindness of Mr. Jodrell:-

"To MR. BRIDGES, at the Bishop of London's, at Fulham.

"SIR,--The favour of your letter, with your remarks, can never be enough acknowledged, and the speed with which you discharged so troublesome a task doubles the obligation.

"I must own you have pleased me very much by the commendations so ill bestowed upon me; but I assure you, much more by the frankness of your censure, which I ought to take the more kindly of the two, as it is more advantage to a scribbler to be improved in his judgment than to be smoothed in his vanity. The greater part of those deviations from the Greek which you have observed I was led into by Chapman and Hobbes; who are, it seems, as much celebrated for their knowledge of the original as they are decried for the badness of their translations. Chapman pretends to have restored the genuine sense of the author from the mistakes of all former explainers in several hundred places; and the Cambridge editors of the large Homer, in Greek and Latin, attributed so much to Hobbes, that they confess they have corrected the old Latin interpretation very often by his version. For my part, I generally took the author's meaning to be as you have explained it; yet their authority, joined to the knowledge of my own imperfectness in the language, overruled me. However, sir, you may be confident, I think you in the right, because you happen to be of my opinion; for men (let them say what they will) never approve any other's sense but as it squares with their own. But you have made me much more proud of and positive in my judgment, since it is strengthened by yours. I think your criticisms which regard the expression very just, and shall make my profit of them; to give you some proof that I am in earnest, I will alter three verses on your bare objection, though I have Mr. Dryden's example for each of them. And this, I hope, you will account no small piece of obedience, from one who values the authority of one true poet above that of twenty critics or commentators. But, though

I speak thus of commentators, I will continue to read carefully all I can procure, to make up that way for my own want of critical understanding in the original beauties of Homer. Though the greatest of them are certainly those of invention and design, which are not at all confined to the language; for the distinguishing excellences of Homer are (by the consent of the best critics of all nations), first in the manners (which include all the speeches, as being no other than the representations of each person's manners by his words): and then in that rapture and fire, which carries you away with him, with that wonderful force, that no man who has a true poetical spirit is master of himself while he reads him. Homer makes you interested and concerned before you are aware, all at once, where Virgil does it by soft degrees. This, I believe, is what a translator of Homer ought principally to imitate; and it is very hard for any translator to come up to it, because the chief reason why all translations fall short of their originals is, that the very constraint they are obliged to renders them heavy and dispirited.

"The great beauty of Homer's language, as I take it, consists in that noble simplicity which runs through all his works (and yet his diction, contrary to what one would imagine consistent with simplicity, is at the same time very copious). I don't know how I have run into this pedantry in a letter, but I find I have said too much, as well as spoken too inconsiderately; what farther thoughts I have upon this subject I shall be glad to communicate to you (for my own improvement) when we meet, which is a happiness I very earnestly desire, as I do likewise some opportunity of proving how much I think myself obliged to your friendship, and how truly I am, sir,

"Your most faithful humble servant,

"A. POPE."

The criticism upon Pope's Epitaphs, which was printed in "The Universal Visitor," is placed here, being too minute and particular to be inserted in the Life.

Every art is best taught by example. Nothing contributes more to the cultivation of propriety than remarks on the works of those who have most excelled. I shall therefore endeavour at this VISIT to entertain the young students in poetry with an examination of Pope's Epitaphs.

To define an epitaph is useless; every one knows that it is an inscription on a tomb. An epitaph, therefore, implies no particular character of writing, but may be composed in verse or prose. It is, indeed, commonly panegyrical, because we are seldom distinguished with a stone but by our friends; but it has no rule to restrain or mollify it except this, that it ought not to be longer than common beholders may be expected to have leisure and patience to peruse.

On CHARLES Earl of DORSET, in the church of Wythyham in Sussex.

> Dorset, the grace of courts, the Muse's pride, Patron of arts, and judge of nature, died. The scourge of pride, though sanctified or great, Of fops in learning, and of knaves in state; Yet soft in nature, though severe his lay, His anger moral, and his wisdom gay. Blest satirist! who touched the means so true, As showed Vice had his hate and pity too. Blest courtier! who could king and country please, Yet sacred kept his friendship and his ease. Blest peer! his great forefathers' every grace Reflecting, and reflected on his race; Where other Buckhursts, other Dorsets shine, And patriots still, or pests, deck the line.

The first distich of this epitaph contains a kind of information which few would want, that the man for whom the tomb was erected DIED. There are indeed some qualities worthy of the praise ascribed to the dead, but none that were likely to exempt him from the lot of man, or incline us much to wonder that he should die. What is meant by "judge of nature" is not easy to say. Nature is not the object of human judgment; for it is in vain to judge where we cannot alter. If by nature is meant what is commonly called NATURE by the critics, a just representation of things really existing, and actions really performed, nature cannot be properly opposed to ART; nature being, in this sense, only the best effect of ART.

The scourge of pride -

Of this couplet the second line is not what is intended, an illustration of the former. PRIDE in the GREAT, is indeed well enough connected with knaves in state, though KNAVES is a word rather too ludicrous and light; but the mention of SANCTIFIED pride will not lead the thoughts to FOPS IN LEARNING, but rather to some species of tyranny or oppression, something more gloomy and more formidable than foppery.

Yet soft his nature -

This is a high compliment, but was not first bestowed on Dorset by Pope. The next verse is extremely beautiful.

Blest satirist! -

In this distich is another line of which Pope was not the author. I do not mean to blame these imitations with much harshness; in long performances they are scarcely to be avoided, and in shorter they may be indulged, because the train of the composition may naturally involve them, or the scantiness of the subject allow little choice. However, what is borrowed is not to be enjoyed as our own, and it is the business of critical justice to give every bird of the Muses his proper feather.

Blest courtier! -

Whether a courtier can properly be commended for keeping his EASE SA-CRED, may perhaps be disputable. To please king and country without sacrificing friendship to any change of times was a very uncommon instance of prudence or felicity, and deserved to be kept separate from so poor a commendation as care of his ease. I wish our poets would attend a little more accurately to the use of the word SACRED, which surely should never be applied in a serious composition, but where some reference may be made to a higher Being, or where some duty is exacted or implied. A man may keep his friendship sacred, because promises of friendship are very awful ties; but methinks he cannot, but in a burlesque sense, be said to keep his ease SACRED.

Blest peer! -

The blessing ascribed to the PEER has no connection with his peerage; they might happen to any other man whose posterity were likely to be regarded.

I know not whether this epitaph be worthy either of the writer or the man entombed.

II.

On Sir WILLIAM TRUMBULL, one of the principal Secretaries of State to King WILLIAM III., who, having resigned his place, died in his retirement at Easthamstead, in Berkshire, 1716.

A pleasing form, a firm, yet cautious mind, Sincere, though prudent; constant, yet resigned; Honour unchanged, a principle profest. Fixed to one side, but moderate to the rest; An honest courtier, yet a patriot too, Just to his prince, and to his country true; Filled with the sense of age, the fire of youth, A scorn of wrangling, yet a zeal for truth; A generous faith, from superstition free; A love to peace, and hate of tyranny; Such this man was; who new from earth removed At length enjoys that liberty he loved.

In this epitaph, as in many others, there appears at the first view a fault which I think scarcely any beauty can compensate. The name is omitted. The end of an epitaph is to convey some account of the dead; and to what purpose is anything told of him whose name is concealed? An epitaph, and a history of a nameless hero, are equally absurd, since the virtues and qualities so recounted in either are scattered at the mercy of fortune to be appropriated by guess. The name, it is true, may be read upon the stone; but what obligation has it to the poet, whose verses wander over the earth and leave their subject behind them, and who is forced, like an unskilful painter, to make his purpose known by adventitious help? This epitaph is wholly without elevation, and contains nothing striking or particular; but the poet is not to be blamed for the defect of his subject. He said perhaps the best that could be said. There are, however, some defects which were not made necessary by the character in which he was employed. There is no opposition between an HONEST COURT-IER and a PATRIOT; for an HONEST, COURTIER cannot but be a PATRIOT. It was unsuitable to the nicety required in short compositions to close his verse with the word TOO; every rhyme should be a word of emphasis: nor can this rule be safely neglected, except where the length of the poem makes slight inaccuracies excusable, or allows room for beauties sufficient to overpower the effects of petty faults.

At the beginning of the seventh line the word FILLED is weak and prosaic, having no particular adaptation to any of the words that follow it. The thought in the last line is impertinent, having no connection with the foregoing character, nor with the condition of the man described. Had the epitaph been written on the poor conspirator who died lately in prison, after a confinement of more than forty years, without any crime proved against him, the sentiment had been just and pathetical; but why should Trumbull be congratulated upon his liberty who had never known restraint?

III.

On the Hon. SIMON HARCOURT, only son of the Lord Chancellor HAR-COURT, at the Church of Stanton-Harcourt in Oxfordshire, 1720.

To this sad shrine, whoe'er thou art, draw near, Here lies the friend most loved, the son most dear; Who ne'er knew joy, but friendship might divide, Or gave his father grief but when he died.   How vain is reason, eloquence how weak! If

Pope must tell what Harcourt cannot speak. Oh let thy once-loved friend inscribe thy stone, And with a father's sorrows mix his own!

This epitaph is principally remarkable for the artful introduction of the name, which is inserted with a peculiar felicity, to which chance must concur with genius, which no man can hope to attain twice, and which cannot be copied but with servile imitation. I cannot but wish that, of this inscription, the two last lines had been omitted, as they take away from the energy what they do not add to the sense.

IV.

On JAMES CRAGGS, Esq., in Westminster Abbey.

JACOBVS CRAGS, REGI MAGNAE BRITANNIAE A SECRETIS ET CONSILIIS SANCTIORIBVS, PRINCIPIS PARITER AC POPVLI AMOR ET DELICIAE: VIXIT TITLIS ET INVIDIA MAJOR ANNOS HEV PAVCOS, XXXV. OB. FEB. XVI. MDCCXX.

Statesman, yet friend to truth; of soul sincere, In action faithful, and in honour clear! Who broke no premise, served no private end, Who gained no title, and who lost no friend; Ennobled by himself, by all approved, Praised, wept, and honoured by the Muse he loved.

The lines on Craggs were not originally intended for an epitaph; and therefore some faults are to be imputed to the violence with which they are torn from the poems that first contained them. We may, however, observe some defects. There is a redundancy of words in the first couplet: it is superfluous to tell of him, who was SINCERE, TRUE, and FAITHFUL, that he was IN HONOUR CLEAR. There seems to be an opposition intended in the fourth line, which is not very obvious: where is the relation between the two positions, that he GAINED NO TITLE and LEST NO FRIEND?

It may be proper here to remark the absurdity of joining in the same inscription Latin and English or verse and prose. If either language be preferable to the other, let that only be used; for no reason can be given why part of the information should be given in one tongue, and part in another on a tomb, more than in any other place, or any other occasion; and to tell all that can be conveniently told in verse, and then to call in the help of prose, has always the appearance of a very artless expedient, or of an attempt unaccomplished. Such an epitaph resembles the conversation of a foreigner, who tells part of his meaning by words, and conveys part by signs.

V.

Intended for Mr. ROWE, in Westminster Abbey.

Thy reliques, Rowe, to this fair urn we trust, And sacred, place by Dryden's awful dust; Beneath a rude and nameless stone he lies, To which thy tomb shall guide inquiring eyes. Peace to thy gentle shade, and endless rest! Blest in thy genius, in thy love too blest; One grateful women to thy fame supplies What a whole thankless land to his denies.

Of this inscription the chief fault is that it belongs less to Rowe, for whom it was written, than to Dryden, who was buried near him; and indeed gives very little information concerning either.

To wish PEACE TO THY SHADE is too mythological to be admitted into a Christian temple: the ancient worship has infected almost all our other compositions, and might therefore be contented to spare our epitaphs. Let fiction, at least, cease with life, and let us be serious over the grave.

VI.

On Mrs. CORBET, who died of a Cancer in her Breast.

Here rests a woman, good without pretence, Blest with plain reason, and with sober sense; No conquest she, but o'er herself, desired; No arts essayed, but not to be admired. Passion and pride were to her soul unknown, Convinced that Virtue only is our own. So unaffected, so composed a mind, So firm, yet soft, so strong, yet so refined, Heaven, as its purest gold, by tortures tried; The saint sustained it, but the woman died.

I have always considered this as the most valuable of all Pope's epitaphs; the subject of it is a character not discriminated by any shining or eminent peculiarities; yet that which really makes, though not the splendour, the felicity of life, and that which every wise man will choose for his final and lasting companion in the languor of age, in the quiet of privacy, when he departs weary and disgusted from the ostentatious, the volatile, and the vain. Of such a character, which the dull overlook and the gay despise, it was fit that the value should be made known and the dignity established. Domestic virtue, as it is exerted without great occasions, or conspicuous consequences, in an even unnoted tenor, required the genius of Pope to display it in such a manner as might attract regard and enforce reverence. Who can forbear to lament that this amiable woman has no name in the verses? If the particular lines of this inscription be examined, it will appear less faulty than the rest. There is scarce one line taken from commonplaces, unless it be that in which ONLY VIRTUE is said to be OUR OWN. I once heard a lady of great beauty and excellence object to the fourth line that it contained an unnatural and incredible panegyric. Of this let the ladies judge.

VII.

On the Monument of the Hon. ROBERT DIGBY, and of his Sister MARY, erected by their Father the Lord DIGBY in the church of Sherborne in Dorsetshire, 1727

Go! fair example of untainted youth, Of modest wisdom, and pacific truth: Composed in sufferings, and in joy sedate, Good without noise, without pretension great Just of thy word, in every thought sincere, Who knew no wish but what the world might hear: Of softest manners, unaffected mind, Lover of peace, and friend of human kind: Go, live! for heaven's eternal year is thine, Go, and exalt thy mortal to divine.   And thou, blest maid! attendant on his doom. Pensive hast followed to the silent tomb, Steered the same course to the same quiet shore, Not parted long, and now to part no more! Go, then, where only bliss sincere is known! Go, where to love and to enjoy are one! Yet take these tears, Mortality's relief, And, till we share your joys, forgive our grief: These little rites a stone, a verse receive. 'Tis all a father, all a friend can give!

This epitaph contains of the brother only a general indiscriminate character, and of the sister tells nothing but that she died. The difficulty in writing epitaphs is to give a particular and appropriate praise. This, however, is not always to be performed, whatever be the diligence or ability of the writer; for the greater part of mankind HAVE NO CHARACTER AT ALL, have little that distinguishes them from others, equally good or bad, and therefore nothing can be said of them which may not be applied with equal propriety to a thousand more. It is indeed no great panegyric that there is enclosed in this tomb one who was born in one year, and died in another; yet many useful and amiable lives have been spent which yet leave little materials for any other memorial. These are however not the proper subjects of poetry; and whenever friendship, or any other motive, obliges a poet to write on such subjects, he must be forgiven if he sometimes wanders in generalities, and utters the same praises over different tombs.

The scantiness of human praises can scarcely be made more apparent than by remarking how often Pope has, in the few epitaphs which he composed, found it necessary to borrow from himself. The fourteen epitaphs which he has written comprise about a hundred and forty lines, in which there are more repetitions than will easily be found in all the rest of his works. In the eight lines which make the character of Digby there is scarce any thought or word which may not be found in the other epitaphs. The ninth line, which is far the strongest and most elegant, is borrowed from Dryden. The conclusion is the same with that on Harcourt, but is here more elegant and better connected.

VIII.

On Sir GODFREY KNELLER, in Westminster Abbey, 1723.

Kneller, by Heaven, and not a master, taught, Whose art was Nature, and whose pictures thought; Now for two ages, having snatched from fate Whate'er was beauteous, or whate'er was great, Lies crowned with Princes, honours, Poets, lays, Due to his merit, and brave thirst of praise. Living, great Nature feared he might outvie Her works; and dying, fears herself may die.

Of this epitaph the first couplet is good, the second not bad, the third is deformed with a broken metaphor, the word crowned not being applicable to the honours or the lays, and the fourth is not only borrowed from the epitaph on Raphael, but of a very harsh construction.

IX.

On General HENRY WITHERS, in Westminster Abbey, 1729.

Here, Withers, rest! thou bravest, gentlest mind, Thy country's friend, but more of human kind. O born to arms! O worth in youth approved! O soft humanity in age beloved! For thee the hardy veteran drops a tear, And the gay courtier feels the sigh sincere   Withers, adieu! yet not will thee remove Thy martial spirit, or thy social love! Amidst corruption, luxury, and rage, Still leave some ancient virtues to our age: Nor let us say (those English glories gone) The last true Briton lies beneath this stone.

The epitaph on Withers affords another instance of commonplaces, though somewhat diversified by mingled qualities, and the peculiarity of a profession. The second couplet is abrupt, general, and unpleasing; exclamation seldom succeeds in our language; and, I think, it may be observed that the particle O! used at the beginning of a sentence, always offends. The third couplet is more happy; the value expressed for him, by different sorts of men, raises him to esteem; there is yet something of the common cant of superficial satirists, who suppose that the insincerity of a courtier destroys all his sensations, and that he is equally a dissembler to the living and the dead. At the third couplet I should wish the epitaph to close, but that I should be unwilling to lose the two next lines, which yet are dearly bought if they cannot be retained without the four that follow them.

X.

On Mr. ELIJAH FENTON, at Easthamstead in Berkshire, 1730.

This modest stone, what few vain marbles can, May truly say, Here lies an honest man: A poet, blest beyond the poet's fate, Whom Heaven kept sacred from the Proud and Great: Foe to loud praise, and friend to learned ease, Content with science in the vale of peace. Calmly he looked on either life, and here Saw nothing to regret or there to fear; From Nature's temperate feast rose satisfied, Thanked Heaven that he lived, and that he died.

The first couplet of this epitaph is borrowed from Crashaw. The four next lines contain a species of praise peculiar, original, and just. Here, therefore, the inscription should have ended, the latter part containing nothing but what is common to every man who is wise and good. The character of Fenton was so amiable, that I cannot forbear to wish for some poet or biographer to display it more fully for the advantage of posterity. If he did not stand in the first rank of genius, he may claim a place in the second; and, whatever criticism may object to his writings, censure could find very little to blame in his life.

XI.

On Mr. GAY, in Westminster Abbey, 1732.

Of manners gentle, of affections mild; In wit, a muse; simplicity, a child: With native humour tempering virtuous rage, Formed to delight at once and lash the age: Above temptation, in a low estate, And uncorrupted, ev'n among the Great: A safe companion and an easy friend, Unbiased through life, lamented in thy end, These are thy honours! not that here thy bust Is mixed with heroes, or with kings thy dust; But that the worthy and the Good shall say, Striking their pensive bosoms--Here lies GAY.

As Gay was the favourite of our author this epitaph was probably written with an uncommon degree of attention, yet it is not more successfully executed than the rest, for it will not always happen that the success of a poet is proportionate to his labour. The same observation may be extended to all works of imagination, which are often influenced by causes wholly out of the performer's power, by hints of which he perceives not the origin, by sudden elevations of mind which he cannot produce in himself, and which sometimes rise when he expects them least. The two parts of the first line are only echoes of each other; GENTLE MANNERS and MILD AFFECTIONS, if they mean anything, must mean the same.

That Gay was a MAN IN WIT is a very frigid commendation; to have the wit of a man is not much for a poet. The WIT OF MAN and the SIMPLICITY OF A CHILD make a poor and vulgar contrast, and raise no ideas of excellence, either intellectual or moral.

In the next couplet RAGE is less properly introduced after the mention of MILDNESS and GENTLENESS, which are made the constituents of his character; for a man so MILD and GENTLE to TEMPER his RAGE was not difficult. The next line is inharmonious in its sound, and mean in its conception; the opposition is obvious, and the word LASH used absolutely, and without any modification, is gross and improper. To be ABOVE TEMPTATION in poverty and FREE FROM CORRUPTION AMONG THE GREAT is indeed such a peculiarity as deserved notice. But to be a SAFE COMPANION is a praise merely negative, arising not from possession of virtue but the absence of vice, and that one of the most odious.

As little can be added to his character by asserting that he was LAMENTED IN HIS END. Every man that dies is, at least by the writer of his epitaph, supposed to be lamented, and therefore this general lamentation does no honour to Gay.

The first eight lines have no grammar; the adjectives are without any substantive, and the epithets without a subject. The thought in the last line, that Gay is buried in the bosoms of the WORTHY and GOOD, who are distinguished only to lengthen the line, is so dark that few understand it, and so harsh, when it is explained, that still fewer approve.

XII.

Intended for Sir ISAAC NEWTON, in Westminster Abbey.

ISAACUS NEWTONIUS: Quem Immortalem Testantur, Tempus, Natura, Coelum: Mortalem hoc marmor fatetur. Nature, and Nature's laws, lay hid in night:

God said, Let Newton be! And all was light.

On this epitaph, short as it is, the faults seem not to be very few. Why part should be Latin and part English it is not easy to discover. In the Latin the opposition of IMMORTALIS and MORTALIS is a mere sound, or a mere quibble; he is not IMMORTAL in any sense contrary to that in which he is MORTAL. In the verses the thought is obvious, and the words NIGHT and LIGHT are too nearly allied.

XIII.

On EDMUND Duke of BUCKINGHAM, who died in the 19th Year of his Age, 1735.

If modest youth, with cool reflection crowned, And every opening virtue blooming round, Could save a parent's justest pride from fate, Or add one patriot to a sinking state; This weeping marble had not asked thy tear, Or sadly told how many hopes lie here! The living virtue now had shone approved, The senate heard him, and his country loved. Yet softer honours, and less noisy fame, Attend the shade of gentle Buckingham: In whom a race, for courage famed and art, Ends in the milder merit of the heart; And, chiefs or sages long to Britain given, Pays the last tribute of a saint to heaven.

This epitaph Mr. Warburton prefers to the rest, but I know not for what reason. To CROWN with REFLECTION is surely a mode of speech approaching to nonsense. OPENING VIRTUES BLOOMING ROUND is something like tautology; the six following lines are poor and prosaic. ART is in another couplet used for ARTS, that a rhyme may be had to HEART. The six last lines are the best, but not excellent.

The rest of his sepulchral performances hardly deserve the notice of criticism. The contemptible dialogue between He and She should have been suppressed for the author's sake.

In his last epitaph on himself, in which he attempts to be jocular upon one of the few things that make wise men serious, he confounds the living man with the dead:

"Under this stone, or under this sill, Or under this turf, &c."

When a man is once buried, the question, under what he is buried, is easily decided. He forgot that though he wrote the epitaph in a state of uncertainty, yet it could not be laid over him till his grave was made. Such is the folly of wit when it is ill employed.

The world has but little new, even this wretchedness seems to have been borrowed from the following tuneless lines:-

"Ludovici Areosti humantur ossa Sub hoc marmore, vel sub hac humo, seu Sub quicquid voluit benignus haeres Siv haerede benignior comes, seu Opportunius incidens Viator: Nam scire haud potuit futura, sed nec Tanti erat vacuum sibi cadaver Ut utnam cuperet parere vivens, Vivens ista tamen sibi paravit. Quae inscribi voluit suo sepulchro Olim siquod haberetis sepulchrum."

Surely Ariosto did not venture to expect that his trifle would have ever had such an illustrious imitator.

The Codes Of Hammurabi And Moses
W. W. Davies

QTY

The discovery of the Hammurabi Code is one of the greatest achievements of archaeology, and is of paramount interest, not only to the student of the Bible, but also to all those interested in ancient history...

Religion   **ISBN:** *1-59462-338-4*   **Pages:132**
MSRP *$12.95*

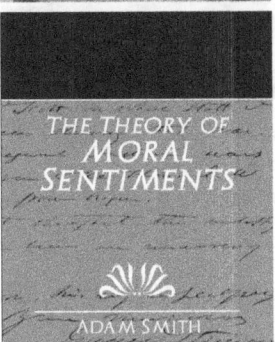

The Theory of Moral Sentiments
Adam Smith

QTY

This work from 1749. contains original theories of conscience amd moral judgment and it is the foundation for systemof morals.

Philosophy **ISBN:** *1-59462-777-0*   **Pages:536**
MSRP *$19.95*

Jessica's First Prayer
Hesba Stretton

QTY

In a screened and secluded corner of one of the many railway-bridges which span the streets of London there could be seen a few years ago, from five o'clock every morning until half past eight, a tidily set-out coffee-stall, consisting of a trestle and board, upon which stood two large tin cans, with a small fire of charcoal burning under each so as to keep the coffee boiling during the early hours of the morning when the work-people were thronging into the city on their way to their daily toil...

Childrens   **ISBN:** *1-59462-373-2*   **Pages:84**
MSRP *$9.95*

My Life and Work
Henry Ford

QTY

Henry Ford revolutionized the world with his implementation of mass production for the Model T automobile. Gain valuable business insight into his life and work with his own auto-biography... "We have only started on our development of our country we have not as yet, with all our talk of wonderful progress, done more than scratch the surface. The progress has been wonderful enough but..."

Biographies/   **ISBN:** *1-59462-198-5*   **Pages:300**
MSRP *$21.95*

The Art of Cross-Examination
Francis Wellman

QTY

I presume it is the experience of every author, after his first book is published upon an important subject, to be almost overwhelmed with a wealth of ideas and illustrations which could readily have been included in his book, and which to his own mind, at least, seem to make a second edition inevitable. Such certainly was the case with me; and when the first edition had reached its sixth impression in five months, I rejoiced to learn that it seemed to my publishers that the book had met with a sufficiently favorable reception to justify a second and considerably enlarged edition. ..

Pages:412

Reference   **ISBN: *1-59462-647-2***   *MSRP $19.95*

On the Duty of Civil Disobedience
Henry David Thoreau

QTY

Thoreau wrote his famous essay, On the Duty of Civil Disobedience, as a protest against an unjust but popular war and the immoral but popular institution of slave-owning. He did more than write—he declined to pay his taxes, and was hauled off to gaol in consequence. Who can say how much this refusal of his hastened the end of the war and of slavery ?

Law   **ISBN: *1-59462-747-9***   **Pages:48**

MSRP $7.45

Dream Psychology Psychoanalysis for Beginners
Sigmund Freud

QTY

Sigmund Freud, born Sigismund Schlomo Freud (May 6, 1856 - September 23, 1939), was a Jewish-Austrian neurologist and psychiatrist who co-founded the psychoanalytic school of psychology. Freud is best known for his theories of the unconscious mind, especially involving the mechanism of repression; his redefinition of sexual desire as mobile and directed towards a wide variety of objects; and his therapeutic techniques, especially his understanding of transference in the therapeutic relationship and the presumed value of dreams as sources of insight into unconscious desires.

Pages:196

Psychology   **ISBN: *1-59462-905-6***   *MSRP $15.45*

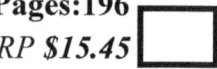

The Miracle of Right Thought
Orison Swett Marden

QTY

Believe with all of your heart that you will do what you were made to do. When the mind has once formed the habit of holding cheerful, happy, prosperous pictures, it will not be easy to form the opposite habit. It does not matter how improbable or how far away this realization may see, or how dark the prospects may be, if we visualize them as best we can, as vividly as possible, hold tenaciously to them and vigorously struggle to attain them, they will gradually become actualized, realized in the life. But a desire, a longing without endeavor, a yearning abandoned or held indifferently will vanish without realization.

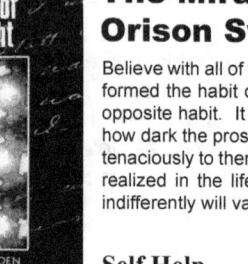

Pages:360

Self Help   **ISBN: *1-59462-644-8***   *MSRP $25.45*

www.bookjungle.com *email: sales@bookjungle.com fax: 630-214-0564 mail: Book Jungle PO Box 2226 Champaign, IL 61825*

QTY

The Rosicrucian Cosmo-Conception Mystic Christianity *by Max Heindel* ISBN: *1-59462-188-8* **$38.95**
The Rosicrucian Cosmo-conception is not dogmatic, neither does it appeal to any other authority than the reason of the student. It is: not controversial, but is: sent forth in the, hope that it may help to clear... New Age/Religion Pages 646

Abandonment To Divine Providence *by Jean-Pierre de Caussade* ISBN: *1-59462-228-0* **$25.95**
"The Rev. Jean Pierre de Caussade was one of the most remarkable spiritual writers of the Society of Jesus in France in the 18th Century. His death took place at Toulouse in 1751. His works have gone through many editions and have been republished... Inspirational/Religion Pages 400

Mental Chemistry *by Charles Haanel* ISBN: *1-59462-192-6* **$23.95**
Mental Chemistry allows the change of material conditions by combining and appropriately utilizing the power of the mind. Much like applied chemistry creates something new and unique out of careful combinations of chemicals the mastery of mental chemistry... New Age Pages 354

The Letters of Robert Browning and Elizabeth Barret Barrett 1845-1846 vol II ISBN: *1-59462-193-4* **$35.95**
*by **Robert Browning** and **Elizabeth Barrett*** Biographies Pages 596

Gleanings In Genesis (volume I) *by Arthur W. Pink* ISBN: *1-59462-130-6* **$27.45**
Appropriately has Genesis been termed "the seed plot of the Bible" for in it we have, in germ form, almost all of the great doctrines which are afterwards fully developed in the books of Scripture which follow... Religion/Inspirational Pages 420

The Master Key *by L. W. de Laurence* ISBN: *1-59462-001-6* **$30.95**
In no branch of human knowledge has there been a more lively increase of the spirit of research during the past few years than in the study of Psychology, Concentration and Mental Discipline. The requests for authentic lessons in Thought Control, Mental Discipline and... New Age/Business Pages 422

The Lesser Key Of Solomon Goetia *by L. W. de Laurence* ISBN: *1-59462-092-X* **$9.95**
This translation of the first book of the "Lemegton" which is now for the first time made accessible to students of Talismanic Magic was done, after careful collation and edition, from numerous Ancient Manuscripts in Hebrew, Latin, and French... New Age/Occult Pages 92

Rubaiyat Of Omar Khayyam *by Edward Fitzgerald* ISBN: *1-59462 332-5* **$13.95**
Edward Fitzgerald, whom the world has already learned, in spite of his own efforts to remain within the shadow of anonymity, to look upon as one of the rarest poets of the century, was born at Bredfield, in Suffolk, on the 31st of March, 1809. He was the third son of John Purcell... Music Pages 172

Ancient Law *by Henry Maine* ISBN: *1-59462-128-4* **$29.95**
The chief object of the following pages is to indicate some of the earliest ideas of mankind, as they are reflected in Ancient Law, and to point out the relation of those ideas to modern thought. Religiom/History Pages 452

Far-Away Stories *by William J. Locke* ISBN: *1-59462-129-2* **$19.45**
"Good wine needs no bush, but a collection of mixed vintages does. And this book is just such a collection. Some of the stories I do not want to remain buried for ever in the museum files of dead magazine-numbers an author's not unpardonable vanity..." Fiction Pages 272

Life of David Crockett *by David Crockett* ISBN: *1-59462-250-7* **$27.45**
"Colonel David Crockett was one of the most remarkable men of the times in which he lived. Born in humble life, but gifted with a strong will, an indomitable courage, and unremitting perseverance... Biographies/New Age Pages 424

Lip-Reading *by Edward Nitchie* ISBN: *1-59462-206-X* **$25.95**
Edward B. Nitchie, founder of the New York School for the Hard of Hearing, now the Nitchie School of Lip-Reading, Inc, wrote "LIP-READING Principles and Practice". The development and perfecting of this meritorious work on lip-reading was an undertaking... How-to Pages 400

A Handbook of Suggestive Therapeutics, Applied Hypnotism, Psychic Science ISBN: *1-59462-214-0* **$24.95**
*by **Henry Munro*** Health/New Age/Health/Self-help Pages 376

A Doll's House: and Two Other Plays *by Henrik Ibsen* ISBN: *1-59462-112-8* **$19.95**
Henrik Ibsen created this classic when in revolutionary 1848 Rome. Introducing some striking concepts in playwriting for the realist genre, this play has been studied the world over. Fiction/Classics/Plays 308

The Light of Asia *by sir Edwin Arnold* ISBN: *1-59462-204-3* **$13.95**
In this poetic masterpiece, Edwin Arnold describes the life and teachings of Buddha. The man who was to become known as Buddha to the world was born as Prince Gautama of India but he rejected the worldly riches and abandoned the reigns of power when... Religion/History/Biographies Pages 170

The Complete Works of Guy de Maupassant *by Guy de Maupassant* ISBN: *1-59462-157-8* **$16.95**
"For days and days, nights and nights, I had dreamed of that first kiss which was to consecrate our engagement, and I knew not on what spot I should put my lips..." Fiction/Classics Pages 240

The Art of Cross-Examination *by Francis L. Wellman* ISBN: *1-59462-309-0* **$26.95**
Written by a renowned trial lawyer, Wellman imparts his experience and uses case studies to explain how to use psychology to extract desired information through questioning. How-to/Science/Reference Pages 408

Answered or Unanswered? *by Louisa Vaughan* ISBN: *1-59462-248-5* **$10.95**
Miracles of Faith in China Religion Pages 112

The Edinburgh Lectures on Mental Science (1909) *by Thomas* ISBN: *1-59462-008-3* **$11.95**
This book contains the substance of a course of lectures recently given by the writer in the Queen Street Hall, Edinburgh. Its purpose is to indicate the Natural Principles governing the relation between Mental Action and Material Conditions... New Age/Psychology Pages 148

Ayesha *by H. Rider Haggard* ISBN: *1-59462-301-5* **$24.95**
Verily and indeed it is the unexpected that happens! Probably if there was one person upon the earth from whom the Editor of this, and of a certain previous history, did not expect to hear again... Classics Pages 380

Ayala's Angel *by Anthony Trollope* ISBN: *1-59462-352-X* **$29.95**
The two girls were both pretty, but Lucy who was twenty-one who supposed to be simple and comparatively unattractive, whereas Ayala was credited, as her Bombwhat romantic name might show, with poetic charm and a taste for romance. Ayala when her father died was nineteen... Fiction Pages 484

The American Commonwealth *by James Bryce* ISBN: *1-59462-286-8* **$34.45**
An interpretation of American democratic political theory. It examines political mechanics and society from the perspective of Scotsman James Bryce Politics Pages 572

Stories of the Pilgrims *by Margaret P. Pumphrey* ISBN: *1-59462-116-0* **$17.95**
This book explores pilgrims religious oppression in England as well as their escape to Holland and eventual crossing to America on the Mayflower, and their early days in New England... History Pages 268

QTY

The Fasting Cure *by Sinclair Upton*　　　　　　　　　　ISBN: *1-59462-222-1*　**$13.95**
In the Cosmopolitan Magazine for May, 1910, and in the Contemporary Review (London) for April, 1910, I published an article dealing with my experiences in fasting. I have written a great many magazine articles, but never one which attracted so much attention... New Age/Self Help/Health Pages 164

Hebrew Astrology *by Sepharial*　　　　　　　　　　　ISBN: *1-59462-308-2*　**$13.45**
In these days of advanced thinking it is a matter of common observation that we have left many of the old landmarks behind and that we are now pressing forward to greater heights and to a wider horizon than that which represented the mind-content of our progenitors... Astrology Pages 144

Thought Vibration or The Law of Attraction in the Thought World　　ISBN: *1-59462-127-6*　**$12.95**
by William Walker Atkinson　　　　　　　　　　　　　　　　　*Psychology/Religion Pages 144*

Optimism *by Helen Keller*　　　　　　　　　　　　ISBN: *1-59462-108-X*　**$15.95**
Helen Keller was blind, deaf, and mute since 19 months old, yet famously learned how to overcome these handicaps, communicate with the world, and spread her lectures promoting optimism. An inspiring read for everyone... Biographies/Inspirational Pages 84

Sara Crewe *by Frances Burnett*　　　　　　　　　　　ISBN: *1-59462-360-0*　**$9.45**
In the first place, Miss Minchin lived in London. Her home was a large, dull, tall one, in a large, dull square, where all the houses were alike, and all the sparrows were alike, and where all the door-knockers made the same heavy sound... Childrens/Classic Pages 88

The Autobiography of Benjamin Franklin *by Benjamin Franklin*　　ISBN: *1-59462-135-7*　**$24.95**
The Autobiography of Benjamin Franklin has probably been more extensively read than any other American historical work, and no other book of its kind has had such ups and downs of fortune. Franklin lived for many years in England, where he was agent... Biographies/History Pages 332

Name	
Email	
Telephone	
Address	
City, State ZIP	

☐ **Credit Card**　　　　　　　☐ **Check / Money Order**

Credit Card Number	
Expiration Date	
Signature	

Please Mail to:　Book Jungle
　　　　　　　　　PO Box 2226
　　　　　　　　　Champaign, IL 61825
or Fax to:　　　　630-214-0564

ORDERING INFORMATION

web*: www.bookjungle.com*
email*: sales@bookjungle.com*
fax*: 630-214-0564*
mail*: Book Jungle PO Box 2226 Champaign, IL 61825*
or PayPal *to sales@bookjungle.com*

Please contact us for bulk discounts

DIRECT-ORDER TERMS

**20% Discount if You Order
Two or More Books**
Free Domestic Shipping!
Accepted: Master Card, Visa,
Discover, American Express